THE MABINOGI

Legend and landscape of Wales

Evening light
across Dyfed from
the Preseli Hills.

THE MABINOGI

Legend
and landscape
of Wales

Translation by:
John K. Bollard

Photography by:
Anthony Griffiths

Published in 2006 by
Gomer Press, Llandysul,
Ceredigion SA44 4JL
www.gomer.co.uk

ISBN 1 84323 348 7
ISBN-13 9781843233480
A CIP record for this title is available
from the British Library

This book is published with the financial support
of the Welsh Books Council.

Designed by Olwen Fowler

Printed and bound in Wales at
Gomer Press, Llandysul, Ceredigion

Pumlumon Moon

To Margaret and Marjorie

Acknowledgements

Before being written, the tales in this book changed and grew as they were passed down over centuries from one storyteller to the next. In an analogous way even today, no book is written just by its author, or in this case, translator. It is moulded and shaped by the many discussions and relationships that an author draws on before and during the actual writing. Thus, I owe thanks to more people than can be named here for their direct and indirect contributions to this book, and those listed below must serve as the representatives of many others. Primary, of course, are the contributions of numerous scholars who have puzzled over, and often solved, many of the difficulties of understanding *The Mabinogi*, in both its language and its cultural setting. In this context, I am particularly indebted to those who introduced me to the rigours and the joys of scholarship as they taught me Middle Welsh. Foremost among these are the late Professor Thomas Jones, Brynley F. Roberts, and J. Beverley Smith, of the Welsh and Welsh History Departments at the University College of Wales, Aberystwyth, more than a few years ago. I have also accrued a considerable indebtedness to many patient friends and colleagues, especially William Oram, Dennis Hudson, David Lloyd, Marged Haycock, John Koch, Edryd Stevens, and Thalia Pandiri. Much of the visual beauty of this book, of course, comes from the hard work and discerning eye of Anthony Griffiths. It is immensely satisfying to work so closely with an old friend, especially one whose attention to detail and, as it turns out, editorial skills nearly match the excellence of his photographs.

In regard to the relationship of *The Mabinogi* to the Welsh landscape and the photographs in

this book, Anthony and I have benefited greatly from the advice of and discussions with David Austin, Ian Hughes, and Jim Perrin. We would also like to thank Catrin Lloyd-Bollard and Brett Brecon for producing such a clear and thorough map of places named in the tales, Sara Kent for her permission to visit and photograph the remains of the enclosure at Camp Hill, and the staff of the Royal Commission on the Ancient and Historical Monuments of Wales in Aberystwyth for making their files available. The staffs of the National Library of Wales and of Jesus College and the Bodleian Library, Oxford, very graciously provided photographs of pages from the medieval manuscripts of the tales.

On a more personal level, Anthony's wife, Marjorie, provided inestimable help, not only by taking notes and keeping records on about 800 photographs from which the ones in this book were selected, but through her welcome assistance and companionship during many hours of trekking and driving around Wales and waiting for just the right photographic moment in all kinds of weather. And throughout the many years I have been engaged with *The Mabinogi*, my wife, Margaret Lloyd, has been a constant support and a patient listener. She has provided more valuable counsel and advice than anyone else will ever know.

Finally, every book needs a scrupulous and demanding editor, and we have been fortunate that our editor, Ceri Wyn Jones, designer Olwen Fowler, and Gomer Press have taken such an interest in this project. We can think of no editor or press better qualified for presenting this translation of *The Mabinogi* to the people of Wales and beyond.

Contents

INTRODUCTION

The Magic and Mystery of *The Mabinogi*

*T*he *Mabinogi*, also known as *The Four Branches of the Mabinogi*, is a set of four interrelated tales widely regarded as the finest example of medieval Welsh prose narrative. Many of the characters and events are drawn from Welsh myth, legend, and lore, from a past much deeper than the period when it was compiled in essentially the form we now have it. But though the storyteller draws on ancient material, the language, culture, and concerns portrayed in these tales are consistent with what we know of Wales in the late eleventh or early twelfth century, when it was written down in a form close to that of the texts surviving in the thirteenth- and fourteenth-century manuscripts. We can be confident, therefore, that these tales entertained and instructed at least some medieval Welsh readers for three hundred years or more. However widely known *The Mabinogi* may have been throughout medieval Wales, its audience certainly included noble men and women – aristocrats and rulers, officers and members of the royal courts and their descendants, whose lives and concerns were similar in many respects to those of the characters we meet here. The continued popularity of *The Mabinogi* since it was rediscovered, published, and translated in the early nineteenth century testifies to its timeless relevance and artistic value, assuring it a respected place among the classics of European literature.

Yet, while it is solidly rooted in the known world, *The Mabinogi* is not entirely of this world; these tales are thoroughly imbued with the magical and otherworldly. Indeed, one of the earliest known modern commentaries on *The Mabinogi* goes so far as to say that it surpasses even the wonders of Greek mythology: 'This author strives, with his creations, to outdo the Chimaera, or whatever monstrous creature all of Greece has to offer.'[1] Many of the characters derive ultimately from much earlier Celtic gods and goddesses, and many of the events and episodes draw on mythologies all but forgotten. As readers or as listeners, we are drawn into an unfamiliar atmosphere where the principles that generally govern life and death may be held in abeyance, where the expectations that we have garnered from our experience are often thwarted, where even the very nature of space and time comes into question. At the same time, however, the events in these tales take place for

[1] This note, written in Latin in a blank space at the end of the Fourth Branch in the 14th-century *White Book of Rhydderch*, states that this is 'the judgement of I.D. about the present author'. I. D. is almost certainly Dr. John Davies of Mallwyd, a scholar and antiquarian who examined the manuscript in 1634 or shortly thereafter. (The Greek *Chimaera* was said to be part lion, part goat, and part serpent.)

the most part within the very real Welsh landscape, and they deal with problems that are very human in nature, if expressed in a context that we now view as fantasy.

How can a work be simultaneously so fantastic and so closely tied to the concrete world in which we live? Why would a storyteller or writer tell these tales, and why do we listen with such fascination? The first step in answering these questions is, of course, to read the stories. But read them neither as a sophisticated, superior, or sceptical modern reader, nor as a child simply fascinated by the unusual and the magical. Rather read them with a questioning mind.

One key to understanding *The Mabinogi* is to recognize that it probes issues of importance to all of us, most especially the matter of distinguishing between right and wrong and behaving accordingly. In tales involving magic (which we too often consign solely to the younger reader), good and evil, right and wrong are often put into clear opposition. Indeed, perhaps we like to read such stories to our children in order to clarify for them moral principles that we ourselves experience as complex and murky. But the moral construct

of *The Mabinogi* is by no means simple, and the point is neither to find a rational explanation for events nor to be satisfied with the mystery unexplored. Quite often the element of magic allows the narrator to set up a situation of considerable human complexity. Issues of behaviour and choice occur frequently throughout these tales, and it is helpful to ask at such moments, 'Why did he do that?', 'Is she right or wrong?', or 'What might be the effect of doing that?' You may get an answer as the story progresses, or you may not. Nevertheless, these tales help us reach an understanding of human behaviour in moments of uncertainty. For example, one of the persistent questions addressed implicitly throughout *The Mabinogi* continues to plague us today: Why are we so caught up in the endless cycle of enmity and strife, war and destruction that we visit upon each other with seemingly inexorable regularity?

A technique helpful in understanding these tales is to compare similar episodes and events with one another. For example, insults or perceived insults are given or received at various points. Counterbalancing the enmities and feuds that result from these insults and offences are a

number of friendships – friendships that get made, broken, or mended, friendships that prolong feuds, and friendships that end or prevent them. Each instance thus provides a different view of the ways in which personal and societal responses redress, minimize, or exacerbate the effects of antisocial, potentially dangerous words and actions. A related theme is that of marriage and the relations between men and women. There is at least one marriage in each of the four branches. Thus we might ask, what does a comparison of these episodes tell us about the narrator's understanding of marriage, and how does that understanding relate to other themes and episodes in *The Mabinogi*?

While the interested reader will find a brief discussion of *The Mabinogi* and its various themes in the Afterword, the important first step is to let the tales provide their own justification as you simply enjoy them. Read *The Mabinogi* not only as literature from which something can be learned, not only in a search for meaning, but also as an exciting and wondrous product of the human imagination that provides us with entertainment today to almost the same degree as it must have done for Welsh audiences nearly a thousand years ago.

The Geography of *The Mabinogi*

Much of the geographical setting of *The Mabinogi* is specific and reflects the known political divisions of Wales in the early medieval period. Indeed, it is this geographical precision that inspired us to include the accompanying photographs of many of the places named in the text. As these photographs reveal, some of these locations remain much as they must have looked to an observer in the Middle Ages; others have changed with the centuries and seem more a part of the modern world than of the past.

Some episodes or events in *The Mabinogi* refer to prehistoric remains in the Welsh countryside that undoubtedly excited the wonder and curiosity of the medieval inhabitants of the land much as they do today. An unimposing, low-lying mound with a squat stone erected in its middle on the banks of the River Alaw provided the storyteller (and perhaps a long line of earlier storytellers) with a location for Branwen's grave, as described in the Second Branch, and that mound could thereafter be pointed to as evidence of the veracity of the tale. That we now identify this as a Bronze Age

Place names
in
THE
MABINOGI

Talebolion
Aber Alaw
Bedd
Branwen
Aberffraw
Arllechwedd
Creuwrion
Arfon
GWYNEDD
Caer Saint
Abermenai
Maenor Goed Alun
Dinas Dinlleu
Nantlleu
Caer Aranrhod
Dol Bebin
Bryn Arien
Caer Dathyl
Maenor Bennardd
Nant
Call
[Llyn y Morynion]
Saith Marchog
Dunoding
Dolbenmaen
Bryn Cyfergyr
Edeirnon
Eifynydd
Maen
Cynfael
Tyfiawg
Penllyn
Y Traeth
Y Felenrhyd
Mawr
Harddlech Mur Castell
Mochnant
Ardudwy
POWYS

WALES

Mochdref
Rhos

Mochdref
Ceri
Elenid
Arwystli
LLOEGR
(ENGLAND)
[Nant y Moch]

[Strata Florida]

CEREDIGION

Gorsedd Arberth?
[Crug Mawr]
Rhuddlan Teifi
SEISSYLLWCH
Hereford
Glyn
Cuch
Preseli

YSTRAD
TYWI

DYFED

Gwales
Arberth
Gorsedd Arberth?

Penfro

GWENT
Is Coed

MORGANNWG

multiple burial mound over three thousand years old need not diminish our appreciation of the site as an evocation of one of the great tragic tales of the Middle Ages.

Some locations in *The Mabinogi* may strike us today as plain or ordinary – insofar as any of the Welsh landscape can be said to be either. The circuitous route taken by Gwydion with a herd of stolen pigs is detailed in the Fourth Branch to explain how various places came to have a name associated with pigs (*moch*), and some of these places are still towns today, if perhaps somewhat larger and dotted with shopping centres or holiday cottages. The current residents of Mochdre near Colwyn Bay on the northern coast may know the story of Gwydion's flight

through their town, but that knowledge is no prerequisite for living there; life simply goes on as it long has. Yet the tale provides a link to a traditional past that is no less meaningful for being mythical, literary, or fictional.

We hope that the photographs in this book will help the reader to visualize the setting for the events in *The Mabinogi* and to understand better how the written work is both drawn from and remains part of the very soil of the country that travellers and poets for the past two hundred and fifty years have insisted on painting with a romantic aura of mystery. This mysterious quality may indeed seem palpable at times, especially at sunset or in the early morning mist, but the landscape of *The Mabinogi* is not romantic in any simple sense; rather it is both down-to-earth and evocative of the unseen. It can be hard to differentiate at times whether the countryside is an embodiment of these tales or the tales are an explanation of the land itself.

A Note on the Translation

Recognizing that any translation is to some degree an interpretation of the original, I have tried to render *The Mabinogi* into standard modern English while staying as close as possible to the meaning, phrasing, and construction of the medieval Welsh text. In other words, this is intended to be a fairly close translation, not a retelling of these tales in my own words. *The Mabinogi* has come down to us, of course, in written form, and there are signs that the tales as we know them may have been composed as written texts. Nevertheless, there is no doubt that the narrator's style draws heavily on the ancient art of oral storytelling. Nor is it hard to believe that even in written form these narratives would have been read aloud from their thirteenth- and fourteenth-century manuscripts to an audience of listeners, or even to one's self. Be that as it may, the storyteller's voice is clearly heard in the Welsh original. Rather than lose the qualities that this voice brings to the narrative, I have chosen to retain some linguistic and stylistic elements that are not usually found in present-day written English.

For example, with a few exceptions where 'and' would result in an awkward or misleading English construction, I have retained the narrator's frequent use of the conjunction *a* or *ac* 'and' (occasionally translated as 'but') to connect

independent clauses or sentences. Though 'and' is not as frequently used as a sentence connector in written English, it is heard often in speech, especially in a narrative context. Particularly in a manuscript tradition which did not have standardized rules for punctuation and capitalization such as we have today, this frequent use of 'and' leaves open to the editor's or translator's judgment even such a basic decision as when to mark the beginning or end of a sentence. However, I believe that if you 'listen' to the narrator's voice as you read, this coordinating or run-on style will come to sound natural and fluid and will bring an immediacy and liveliness to the telling. Furthermore, the frequent use of 'and' is not simply a reflection of the oral background of *The Mabinogi*; it is an inherent element of the narrator's style, in which events are simply described in natural sequence. Rather than imply causation or a hierarchy of importance through the dependence of one sentence upon another, the narrator presents us with a straightforward narration of the outward events of the tales and leaves it to us to determine the significance of their relationships. This mode of narration is not unlike that of the original Hebrew texts of the Pentateuch or Torah, in which a similar conjunctive particle simply joins one statement to the next, both setting the pace and requiring the reader himself or herself to reach a deeper understanding.[2]

The medieval Welsh storyteller's art was polished and refined over years of training, and it was highly respected, as is noted in the Fourth Branch itself:

> Gwydion himself was the best tale teller in the world, and that night he entertained the court with pleasant conversation and tales, so that it was praiseworthy to all of the court, and Pryderi was pleased to converse with him.

Thus, we should not expect these tales to be told in an ordinary conversational tone. A skilled storyteller draws us into a tale through a command of language and style that transcends that of everyday usage. The import and the significance, the seriousness and the humour of these tales are conveyed as much by the way in which they are told as by the events that are recounted.

Every language has some features that are difficult to translate. In Welsh, for example, there is a wider range of personal pronouns than

[2] See Robert Alter, *The Art of Biblical Narrative* (1982) and *Genesis: Translation and Commentary* (1996).

in English. The variety of pronouns gives the Welsh reader or listener clues to the emphasis and even the intent or meaning of a phrase or sentence. For example, the simple pronouns for 'he' and 'she' are *ef* and *hi*, but there are also the forms *yntau* and *hithau*. These conjunctive pronouns, as they are called, also mean 'he' and 'she,' but they are more emphatic and, depending on the context, they can carry shades of meaning that might be translated as 'he also,' 'she for her part,' 'but he,' or 'while she'. The present translation generally avoids such expansive renderings, except occasionally where the context demands some elaboration in English in order to clarify the meaning. In one frequently occurring situation, however, I indicate syntactically the note of emphasis that these pronouns carry. In Middle Welsh prose *heb ef* and *heb hi* are the most common ways to say simply 'he said' and 'she said.' *Heb yntau* and *heb hithau* express more emphasis, though often only slight, at times quietly signalling a change of speaker. To reproduce their effect in Welsh, these phrases have usually been translated with the more literary 'said he' and 'said she'.

This inversion may sound a bit old-fashioned or formal to a modern ear – and that is exactly the point; it thereby conveys something of the subtle shifts that a live storyteller communicates through tone, inflection, or loudness, but that are often lost in English on the written page. This formal usage, which may also be apparent here in other ways, might serve as a reminder that *The Mabinogi* is not narrated in a purely conversational style, though it generally has a natural, easy flow. The language is that of a narrative tradition drawn from an oral style based on normal speech patterns but that is more carefully crafted than daily speech. The oral storyteller's diction has been further polished within a written tradition that had developed a fine sense of gradations of style and formality. But unlike the flamboyant artistry of some other medieval Welsh tales, as in the exuberant *Culhwch and Olwen* and the highly rhetorical *Dream of Rhonabwy*, the language of *The Mabinogi* is so carefully crafted, skillfully honed, and gently understated that we scarcely notice its artistry, as if the narrator were abiding by the advice of an early Welsh proverb: *Keluyd kelet y aruaeth*, 'Let the skilful conceal his design.'

John K. Bollard
Florence, Massachusetts

Photographer's Note

A chance meeting with John in Aberystwyth a few years ago resulted in this collaboration. I knew John in the late 1960s when he was a graduate student at the University, and it was our love of folk music, especially the guitar, that brought us together. We only met rarely after this, so I was delighted when he asked me to illustrate his new translation of *The Mabinogi*.

This has been a fascinating project, taking me to many parts of my native Wales that I might not otherwise have visited. I believe I photographed or at least visited nearly all the known Welsh locations mentioned in *The Mabinogi*, and several others, such as Llantarnam and Maen Dylan, not mentioned specifically but associated with the tales. Apart from two taken from the Herefordshire border, all the photographs in this book were taken in Wales.

It has been quite a challenge. Some places had intrusive objects such as pylons, farm sheds, and power stations, which I have done my best to avoid, whilst other areas, especially in the north-west of Wales, lent themselves to landscape photography. It was often difficult determining the whereabouts of some locations. When enquiring of local people, I found more than once that those who knew had differing opinions of where a particular site might be found.

Looking back, certain memorable days stand out – sheltering under a hawthorn bush in a hailstorm at Tomen Y Mur; our first view of the Pembrokeshire islands; sitting on the summit of Carningli watching the moon rise as the sun set; and patiently waiting at Dinas Dinlle hillfort, when, at low tide, the rocks of Caer Arianrhod appeared.

My equipment was a trusty manual Olympus OM1n, with 3 lenses, a 28mm, 35-70 zoom and a 75-150 zoom, with a skylight and a polarising filter. The slide film was Fuji Velvia 50, and every shot was taken on a very reliable tripod.

I would like to thank my wife, Marjorie, who accompanied and assisted me. I would also like to thank all the people I met: landowners, farmers, local residents, and others, who were very helpful with directions and information, and who allowed me access to various sites.

I hope my photography will enhance the enjoyment of *The Mabinogi* and perhaps inspire the reader to visit these places, which still exist in this wonderful small land of Wales.

Anthony Griffiths
Aberystwyth

GENEALOGIES

The Principal Families of *The Mabinogi*

The names of characters appearing in the tales are in boldface type.

Female names are in italic type.

'=' denotes a marriage;

'≈' denotes an illicit or irregular union.

Raised numbers indicate the order of marriages or relationships, where known.

Siblings are not necessarily in order of age.

Casnar Wledig
|
Gloyw Wallt Lydan
|
Gwyn Gohoyw

Hefeydd the Old
|
Pwyll = ¹*Rhiannon*² = **Manawydan**
(see below)

Cigfa = **Pryderi**

Mynogan
|
Beli

Llŷr = *Penarddun* = Euroswydd   **Caswallawn**

Matholwch = *Branwen*   **Manawydan** = *Rhiannon*   **Bendigeidfran**   **Nisien**   **Efnisien**
(see above)

Gwern

Cradawg

Mathonwy

Pebin   *Dôn*
|

Math = ²*Goewin*¹ ≈ ¹**Gilfaethwy**² ≈ **Gwydion**   *Aranrhod*   Gofannon

Bleiddwn **Hyddwn** **Hychdwn Hir**   **Dylan** **Lleu** = ¹*Blodeuedd*² ≈ **Gronw**
                                          Llaw   **Bebr**
                                          Gyffes

The White Book of Rhydderch, NLW Peniarth MS 4, folio 1r. (*By kind permission of the National Library of Wales*).

Pwyll pendeuic dyuet a oed yn arglwyd ar seith chantref dyuet. A th;eig ;....... y doed yn arberth prif lys idav ad;niot ;n;. urist ac y;b uedbl ;;met y hela. Sef kynteir o;g;noeth au;nner y hela gl;nu aith. Ac ef ag;ch o;nnbys y nos honno o arberth ac a doeth hyt ;m ;ein llbyn diarb;a. Ac yno y bu y nos honno. A th; annoeth ;n ;eueugt;t y d;d k;nodi aoruc ad;niot y l;nn cuch ; ellong egbn dau y; wet. A chanu y go;n a doeth ;eu d; g;no; ;; hela. A cherdet ;n ol y ;obn ac y; ;ugolli a; g;d; ;ndeithou. Ac ual y b;d ;n ;m;ar andab allef y; ercho; ;s. ef ag; be; llef erchb;s arall. ac ;;t oed;nt ;mllef. a th;nn ;; ;n d;niot ;n erb;n y erchb;s ef. ac ef a belei la nuerch y;; wet o naes gu astat. ac ual y; d oed y erchb;s ef y;n ;mgael ac ;ft;;s y llan nerch ef a belei carb o; laeu ;; erchb;s arall. a pharth a p;; erued y llan nerch ll;ma ;; erchb;s a oed ;n;; ol ;n ;mo;dibes a; ef. ac ;n;; nbd ;; llab;. ac ;ma ed;;ch o;on ab ef ar lib ;; erchb;s heb h anbb;llab ed;;ch ar ;; carb. ac o; a bel;ei ef o;elg bn y b;;t. n;; bel;ei con ;n llib ar b;nt. Sef llib oed a;nn;t. d acrb;n

llathre;; a; en ckull;au; goch;ou. a; ual y llath; b ;;nuei ;;on s llath;es ; chet y ckull;en. a; ar h;;n; at y;b;; ; deth ef ;e c;;es ;; erchb;s ala d ;iler ; au; e;;ndeith. a llith;ab ;; erchb ;s ch;nan ar ;; carb. a; ual y b;d ;n llath;au ; con. e;b; belei uarchauc ;n d;nu;t ;n ol ;; erchb;s ; a;n;;; erch las mab; a cho;n;;u; am ;n; nb;;l. a g;b;;; th;;n llb;t tei a;nda;; ;n bi;e hela. ac ar h; ;; march abe a doet h; a d;bedut ual ;;unben heb ef ;; b;tti ac n;; ch;; ;t. ;e heb ef a ca; a;uat o au;;;ed ;; h;e;. ;;noer heb e; h;gdabt u; am;;ed aith; e;;eil aun h;nn ;;. a un ;; heb ;n;teu beth d;;;;;. ;rof; a dub h;ep ;n;teu d; an b;;bot d; hun ath; an;; oerb;;t. ;a an;; b erb;t a; ben a belei;t ti a mat ... belei;s au;;;erb;;t ;;e; ;; o; hep ef no g;en;;; ;;; o;;e ala d ;iler ;nau; e;n; e;th. a llith;au o;; erch;b;;; d; l;;namab. h;nn ;; h;e; ef an;;;erb;;t oed. a g;;; n;;t ;nidiall ;; ath;; a dub he;; ef ;n; ab;; an;lot ;tt guert;;

Arberth (Narberth). An Anglo-Norman castle was built in the 13th century on what is the most likely site of the earlier court of Arberth.

[1] *Pwyll Prince of Dyfed:* The Welsh noun *pwyll* means 'wisdom, understanding, discretion.' Pwyll's title *pendefig,* 'chief ruler, prince', is relatively rare in early Welsh, elsewhere occurring primarily in poetry, but not in historical or legal documents.

[2] *cantref:* a division of land in medieval Wales traditionally containing about 100 settlements or large farms, similar to the Anglo-Saxon 'hundred'; from *cant* 'hundred' + *tref* 'town'.

[3] The most likely location is the town of Arberth in Dyfed. (English, Narberth, from *yn Arberth* 'in Arberth'). For the meaning of the name, see note 49 below.

[4] The location of Penn Llwyn Diarwya is unknown.

here begins THE MABINOGI

PWYLL Prince of Dyfed[1] was lord over the seven cantrefs[2] of Dyfed. And once upon a time he was at Arberth, a chief court of his,[3] and it came into his mind and thought to go hunting. This is the part of his realm he wished to hunt – Glyn Cuch. And he set out that night from Arberth, and he came as far as Penn Llwyn Diarwya, and he stayed there that night.[4]

Glyn Cuch
(Cwm Cych).
The upper reaches
of Cwm Cych, still
a pleasant wooded
valley (*glyn*) in
northeastern
Dyfed.

[5] *glyn* 'valley, glen'. The river Cuch, in northeastern Dyfed, flows north into the Teifi.

[6] The term *unben*, 'chieftain,' is used in Middle Welsh prose tales, not strictly as a title, but as a polite form of address.

[7] *Annwn* or *Annwfn*, the otherworld. The root of this name, *dwfn*, could mean either 'deep' (adjective); 'the deep, abyss' (noun); or 'world, earth' (noun). The prefix *an-* may mean 'not, un-' or 'in,' or it may be an intensifying prefix. Thus, *Annwn* has been explained variously to mean 'the very deep, the abyss,' 'the un-world, the other world,' or 'the inner world,' that is, another world, either one beneath the earth, entered through mounds, hills, caves, or lakes as in much Celtic folklore, or one coterminous with our own world, but hidden and reached by magical or mysterious ways.

And the next day, when the day was still young, he arose and came to Glyn Cuch to loose his dogs into the wood.[5] And he sounded his horn and began to muster the hunt, and he became separated from his companions. And as he was listening to the cry of the pack of hounds, he could hear the cry of another pack, and they did not have the same cry, and those were coming toward his pack. And he could see a clearing in the wood, like a level field. And as his pack was reaching the edge of the clearing, he could see a stag before the other pack. And toward the middle of the clearing, behold, the pack which was behind it overtaking it and throwing it to the ground.

And then he looked at the colour of the pack, without bothering to look at the stag. And whatever he had seen of hunting hounds in the world, he had not seen hounds the same colour as they. This is the colour that was on them – shining white, and their ears red. And as the white of the hounds shone, so shone the red of their ears.

And upon that, he came to the hounds and

drove away the pack that had killed the stag and fed his own hounds on the stag. And as he was feeding the hounds, he could see a rider coming after the pack on a great dapple-grey horse, with a hunting horn about his neck and clothing of brownish grey material about him as a hunting garb.

And upon that, the rider came to him and spoke thus to him: 'Ah, chieftain,' he said, 'I know who you are, but I will not greet you.'[6]

'Yea,' he said, 'perhaps you are of such rank that you are not obliged to.'

'God knows,' he replied, 'it is not the dignity of my rank that restrains me in regard to that.'

'Ah, chieftain,' he said, 'what otherwise?'

'Between me and God,' he said, 'your own lack of manners and your discourtesy.'

'What discourtesy, chieftain, did you see in me?'

'I have not seen greater discourtesy in a man,' he said, 'than driving away the pack that had killed the stag and feeding your own pack upon it. That,' he said, 'was discourtesy. And though I will not avenge myself upon you, between me and God,' he said, 'I will do dishonour to you to the value of a hundred stags.'

'Ah, chieftain,' he replied, 'if I have done wrong, I will purchase your friendship.'

'How,' he asked, 'will you purchase it?'

'According to what your rank may be, but I do not know who you are.'

'A crowned king am I in the country I come from.'

'Lord,' he said, 'good day to you. And what country do you come from?'

'From Annwn,' he said. 'Arawn King of Annwn am I!'[7]

'Lord,' he asked, 'how will I get your friendship?'[8]

'Here is how you will get it,' he said. 'There is a man whose realm is next to my realm who is continually warring against me. He is Hafgan, a king of Annwn. And for ridding me of that oppression – and you can do that easily – you will receive my friendship.'

'I will do that,' he said, 'gladly. But tell me how I can do that.'

'I will,' he said. 'Here is how you can do it. I will make a strong friendship with you. This is what I will do – I will place you in my stead in Annwn and I will place the fairest woman you have ever seen to sleep with you every night, with my face and my form upon you so that there will be no chamberlain, no officer, nor other man of those that follow me who will ever know that you are not I. And that,' he said, 'until the end of a year from tomorrow, and we will meet then in this place.'

'Yea,' he asked, 'though I be there until the end of the year, what guidance will I have for finding the man you speak of?'

'A year,' he said, 'from tonight there is a meeting between him and me at the ford. And you be there in my shape,' he said, 'and one blow shall you give him. He will not live from that. And though he may ask you to give a second, do not give it, however he may entreat you. Whatever else I may do to him, the next day he would fight against me as well as before.'

'Yea,' asked Pwyll, 'what will I do with my realm?'

'I will bring it about,' said Arawn, 'that there will be in your kingdom no man nor woman

[8] Pwyll does not admit to doing wrong, but says, 'If I have done wrong...' The medieval Welsh laws suggest that he may not have committed an offence: 'If it happens that a person goes hunting and looses his hounds on an animal, then if idle hounds meet it and kill it, the animal will belong to the first hounds, which started it, unless the idle hounds belong to the King' (Dafydd Jenkins, *Hywel Dda: The Law* [1986], p. 186). However, it is not certain that Pwyll's status as *pendefig* (see note 1) accords him the full legal rights of a king (*brenin*); on the other hand, Arawn is a crowned king (*brenin*), but not of Dyfed, where the animal was taken.

Annwn. The falls and pool of Ffynone on the river Dulas, which flows into the Cych, are reputed locally to be an entrance into the otherworld of Annwn.

who will know that I am not you, and I will go in your stead.'

'Gladly,' said Pwyll, 'will I go.'

'Your way will be unimpeded, and nothing will hinder you until you come to my realm, and I will be your guide.'

He guided him until he saw the court and the settlement. 'There,' he said, 'the court and the realm under your authority. And go to the court. There is no one in it who will not know you. And as you observe the service in it, you will know the custom of the court.'

He made his way to the court, and in the court he could see sleeping quarters and halls and chambers and the fairest adornment of buildings anyone had ever seen. And he went to the hall to take off his boots. There came youths and young servants to remove his boots, and all greeted him as they came. Two knights came to take his hunting garment from him and to put on him a golden garment of silk brocade. And the hall was prepared. There he could see the household troops and hosts, and the most beautiful and best equipped host anyone had ever seen coming in, and the queen with them – the fairest woman anyone had ever seen, with a golden garment of shining silk brocade about her.

And upon that, they went to wash, and they approached the tables, and they sat like this – the queen on one side of him and the earl, he supposed, on the other side. And he began to converse with the queen. And whatever he had experienced conversing with a woman, she was the most natural and the most gracious in her demeanour and her conversation. And they passed the time with food and drink and song and revelry. And whatever he had seen of all the courts in the world, that was the court most abundant in food and drink and gold plate and royal jewels.

The time came for them to go to sleep, and to

sleep they went, he and the queen. As soon as they got in the bed, he turned his face to the edge of the bed and his back toward her. From then until the next day, he did not speak to her a single word. The next day, there was tenderness and amiable conversation between them. Whatever affection may have been between them by day, not a single night until the end of the year was different from the first night.

He spent the year with hunting and song and revelry and affection and conversing with companions, until the night the combat would be. At the appointed time that night, the meeting came as clearly to the memory of the most distant man in the whole realm as to himself. And he came to the meeting, and the noblemen of his realm with him.

And as soon as he came to the ford, a knight rose up and spoke thus: 'Ah, nobles,' he said, 'listen well! This meeting is between the two kings, and that between their own two bodies. And each one of them is a claimant upon the other, and that for land and earth.[9] And each of you must remain still, but let it be between the two of them.'

And upon that the two kings approached each other at the middle of the ford to encounter. And at the first onset, the man who was in Arawn's place struck Hafgan in the centre of the boss of his shield, so that it split in two halves, and so that all the armour broke, and so that Hafgan was the length of his arm and his spear over the hindquarters of his horse to the ground, with a mortal blow upon him.

'Ah, chieftain,' asked Hafgan, 'what right did you have to my death? I was not claiming

anything against you. I do not know, either, a reason for you to slay me, but by God,' he said, 'since you have begun my death – finish!'

'Ah, chieftain,' he replied, 'it could be that I will have regret for doing what I have done to you. Seek who may slay you; I will not slay you.'

'My true nobles,' said Hafgan, 'take me from here. My death is accomplished. I have no means to support you any longer.'

'My nobles,' said the man who was in Arawn's place, 'consult among you and find out who ought to be as vassals to me.'

'Lord,' responded the nobles, 'all are obliged to it, since there is no king over all Annwn except you.'

'Yea,' he said, 'whoever comes submissively, it is right to accept him. Whoever does not come obediently, let him be compelled by force of swords.'

And upon that, he accepted the homage of the men and began to take possession of the land. And by midday the next day, the two kingdoms were in his power.

And upon that, he made his way to his meeting, and he came to Glyn Cuch. And when he arrived there, Arawn was before him. Each one was glad to see the other.

'Yea,' said Arawn, 'may God repay you your friendship; I have heard of it.'

'Yea,' he replied, 'when you come yourself to your land, you will see what I have done for you.'

'What you have done,' he said, 'for me, may God repay it to you.'

Then Arawn gave his own form and

[9] *tir a daear* 'land and earth' is a common legal phrase in medieval Welsh law; its use here indicates that this encounter is to resolve a dispute over territorial rights.

appearance to Pwyll Prince of Dyfed, and he took his own form and appearance.

And Arawn went on toward his court in Annwn, and he rejoiced to see his retinue and his household troop, since he had not seen them for a long time. They, however, had not missed him, and his coming was no more novel than before. That day he spent in pleasure and joy, and sitting and conversing with his wife and his nobles.

And when it was more timely for them to take sleep than revelry, they went to sleep. He went to his bed and his wife came to him. First he conversed with his wife and he engaged in affectionate pleasure and love with her. And she had not been accustomed to that for a year, and she thought about that.

'Oh God,' she said, 'what different thought is in him tonight than what has been for a year until tonight?' And she meditated for a long while. And after that meditation, he awoke, and he said something to her, and a second time, and a third. But he got no answer to that from her.

'Why,' he asked, 'don't you speak to me?'

'I will tell you,' she answered. 'I have not spoken so much for a year in such a place as this.'

'Why?' he said. 'We talked together constantly.'

'Shame on me,' she said, 'if there has been between us for a year from last night, from the time we would go into the folds of the bedclothes, either pleasure, or conversation, or you turned your face toward me, much less what might be more than that.'

And then he thought, 'By the Lord God,' he said, 'a man uniquely strong in friendship, and

steadfast, have I got as a friend.' And then he said to his wife, 'Lady,' he said, 'do not blame me. Between me and God,' he said, 'I have not slept nor have I lain down with you for a year from last night.' And then he told the whole adventure to her.

'To God I make my confession,' she said, 'a strong hold you had on a friend in regard to fighting with the temptation of the flesh and keeping faith with you.'

'Lady,' he replied, 'I was having that same thought when I was silent toward you.'

'That was no wonder,' she said.

Pwyll Prince of Dyfed came to his realm and his land and began to inquire of the nobles of his land what had been his lordship over them that year, compared to what it had been before that.

'Lord,' they said, 'your courtesy was never as good; you yourself were never as pleasant a youth; it was never as easy for you to spend your wealth; your decisions were never better than this year.'

'Between me and God,' he declared, 'it is right for you to thank the man who was with you. And here is the adventure as it was –,' and Pwyll related it all to them.

'Yea, lord,' they said, 'thank God you have got that friendship. And the lordship we have received this year, you will not take it back from us, surely.'

'I will not, between me and God,' said Pwyll.

And from then on they began to strengthen the friendship between them and to send each other horses and hounds and hawks and every kind of jewel which each one supposed would

[10] No certain location for Gorsedd Arberth has been identified; the remains of an Iron-Age enclosure on Camp Hill, overlooking the road less than a mile south of Arberth, provide the most geographically suitable location. Though now barely visible after centuries of ploughing, the enclosure would have been much more prominent in the Middle Ages. Several similar sites in the area are also possibilities. A large hill or mound just north of Aberteifi / Cardigan has also been suggested, but (a) this has been known as Crug Mawr (The Great Hill or

Gorsedd Arberth. The curves of the ramparts, now barely visible, of the circular Iron-Age enclosure at Camp Hill, just south of Narberth, mark the nearest and best located of several possible sites of Gorsedd Arberth. A tower of the medieval castle can be seen to the right, with the town behind.

Cairn) at least since the early ninth century, (b) it would require a different location for Arberth, and (c) it is not in the historical realm of Dyfed; see photo on p. 45. Though there is a stream called Nant Arberth just to the east of Crug Mawr, locating the court of Arberth so close to Glyn Cuch would not fit the geography of the tale. *Gorsedd*, 'mound (of earth), barrow, tumulus, a (prehistoric) burial mound,' also means 'throne' and 'assembly, court.' The root -*sedd* derives from the Indo-European *sed-, also seen in Latin *sedeo* 'I sit' and English *sit* and *seat*.

please the thought of the other. And because of his stay that year in Annwn, and ruling there so successfully, and uniting the two kingdoms as one through his bravery and his prowess, his name, Pwyll Prince of Dyfed, fell out of use, and he was called Pwyll Head of Annwn from then on.

And once upon a time he was at Arberth, a chief court of his, with a feast prepared for him and great hosts of men with him. And after the first serving, Pwyll arose to take a walk, and he made for the top of a mound which was above the court, which was called Gorsedd Arberth.[10]

'Lord,' said one of the court, 'a peculiarity of the mound is, any nobleman whatsoever who sits upon it will not go from there without one of two things — either a wound or blows or he will see a wonder.'

'I have no fear of receiving a wound or blows in the midst of such a host. A wonder, however — I would be pleased to see that. I will go,' he said, 'to the mound to sit.'

He sat on the mound. And as they were sitting, they could see a woman on a great tall pale white horse, with a shining golden garment of silk brocade about her, coming along the highway which went past the mound. Her horse had a slow, steady pace, in the mind of anyone who saw it, and it was coming alongside the mound.

'Ah, men,' asked Pwyll, 'is there any among you who recognizes the horsewoman?'

'No, lord,' they replied.

25

'Let someone go,' he said, 'to meet her to find out who she is.'

One rose up, and when he came to the road to meet her, she had gone past. He pursued her as fast as he could on foot, but the greater his speed would be, the farther she would be from him. And when he saw that it would not prosper him to pursue her, he returned to Pwyll and said to him, 'Lord,' he said, 'it will not prosper anyone in the world on foot to pursue her.'

'Yea,' said Pwyll, 'go to the court and take the swiftest horse you know of, and go forth after her.'

He took the horse and forth he went. He reached the level open ground and he showed the spurs to the horse. But the more he struck the horse, the farther she would be from him. She had the same pace with which she had begun. His horse grew tired, and when he noticed that his horse was tiring to a walk, he returned to where Pwyll was.

'Lord,' he said, 'it will not prosper anyone to pursue the lady yonder. I do not know of a faster horse in the realm than that, and it did not prosper me to pursue her.'

'Yea,' said Pwyll, 'there is some magic intent there. Let us go to the court.'

They came to the court and spent that day. And on the next day, they rose up and spent that until it was time to go to eat. And after the first serving, 'Yea,' said Pwyll, 'let us go, the company that we were yesterday, to the top of the mound. And you,' he said to one of his youths, 'bring with you the swiftest horse that you know of in the field.' And the youth did that.

They went to the mound, and the horse with them. And as they were sitting, they could see the woman on the same horse, with the same garment about her, coming along the same road.

'Behold,' said Pwyll, 'the horsewoman of yesterday. Be ready, lad,' he said, 'to find out who she is.'

'Lord,' he replied, 'I will do that gladly.'

Upon that, the horsewoman came level with them. This is what the youth did then – he mounted the horse. But before he had settled himself in the saddle, she had gone past, with a gap between them. She had a pace no different than the day before. He put his horse to an amble, and he supposed that however slowly his horse went, he would catch up with her. But that did not prosper him. He loosed his horse by the reins. He was no nearer to her then than if he had been at a walk. And the more he struck his horse, the farther she would be from him. Her pace was no greater than before. Since he did not see that it would prosper him to pursue her, he returned and came to where Pwyll was.

'Lord,' he said, 'the horse has no ability other than what you saw.'

'I saw,' he said. 'It will not prosper anyone to follow her. And between me and God,' he declared, 'she had an errand with some in this field, if she would leave her obstinacy to say it. But let us go toward the court.'

They came to the court, and they spent that night in songs and revelry, as it was pleasing to them. And the next day, they enjoyed the day until it was time to go to eat. And when they had finished the food, Pwyll said, 'Where is the company that we were yesterday and the day before on top of the mound?'

'Here, lord,' they answered.

'Let us go,' he said, 'to the mound to sit. And you,' he said to his groom, 'saddle my horse well and bring him to the road, and bring my spurs with you.' The groom did that.

They came to the mound to sit. They were there hardly any time at all until they could see the horsewoman coming along the same road, and in the same form, and at the same pace.

'Ha, lad!' said Pwyll, 'I see the horsewoman. Give me my horse!' Pwyll mounted on his horse.

Gorsedd Arberth. The upper field of Camp Hill (Gorsedd Arberth?), viewed from the ruins of Narberth Castle.

But no sooner does he mount his horse than she goes past him. He turned after her and he allowed his spirited, prancing horse its own pace. And he supposed that at the second leap, or at the third, he would overtake her. He was no nearer to her, however, than before. He spurred on his horse to the fastest pace it had. But he saw it would not prosper him to pursue her.

Then Pwyll said, 'Ah maiden,' he said, 'for the sake of the man you love most, wait for me!'

'I will, gladly,' she said, 'and it would have been better for the horse if you had asked it a good while ago.'

The maiden stood and waited, and drew

back the part of her headdress which ought to be about her face and fixed her gaze upon him and began to converse with him.

'Lady,' he asked, 'where do you come from and what journey are you on?'

'Travelling on my own errands,' she answered, 'and I am pleased to see you.'

'My welcome to you,' he said. And then he thought that unlovely to him was the face of every maiden and woman he had ever seen, compared to her face. 'Lady,' he asked, 'will you tell me anything of your errands?'

'I will, between me and God,' she said. 'My chief errand was to try to see you.'

'That,' said Pwyll, 'is to me the best errand for you to come on. And will you tell me who you are?'

'I will, lord,' she replied. 'I am Rhiannon daughter of Hefeydd the Old, and I am being given to a man against my will.[11] But I have not desired any man, and that is for love of you. And I will not desire it even now, unless you reject me. And I have come to find out your response to that.'

'Between me and God,' declared Pwyll, 'here is my response to you. If I had a choice of all the women and maidens in the world, it is you I would choose.'

'Yea,' she said, 'if that is what you desire, before I am given to another man, make an appointment with me.'

'The sooner,' said Pwyll, 'the better, in my opinion. And in the place which you desire, make the appointment.'

'I will, lord,' she said. 'A year from tonight in the court of Hefeydd, I will bring it about

that there will be prepared a feast ready for your arrival.'

'Gladly,' he said, 'and I will be at that meeting.'

'Lord,' she said, 'farewell, and remember to fulfil your promise. And I will depart now.'

And they separated, and he went toward his household troops and his retinue. Whatever questions they had about the maiden, he would turn to other matters.

They spent the year from then until the time came, and Pwyll equipped himself as one of a hundred knights. He went to the court of Hefeydd the Old. And he came to the court, and they welcomed him, and a great gathering and gladness and provisions were there to greet him, and all the treasures of the court were dispensed according to his counsel. The hall was prepared and they went to the tables. This is how they sat – Hefeydd the Old on one side of Pwyll and Rhiannon on his other side; after that, each one according to his rank. They ate and drank and conversed.

And at the beginning of the revelry after the meal, they could see coming in a large, regal, auburn-haired youth, with a garment of silk brocade about him. And when he came to the upper end of the hall, he greeted Pwyll and his companions.

'God's welcome to you, friend, and come to sit,' said Pwyll.

'I will not,' he replied. 'I am a suppliant and I will do my errand.'

'Do it gladly,' said Pwyll.

'Lord,' he said, 'my errand is to you, and I have come to make a request of you.'

[11] The name Rhiannon derives from an earlier Celtic form *Rigantona*, 'divine queen'; her mythological origins are evidenced in her various magical attributes throughout the First Branch.

'Whatever request you ask of me, as long as I am able to obtain it, it shall be yours.'

'Alas!' said Rhiannon. 'Why do you give an answer in such a way?'

'He has given it thus, lady, in the presence of noblemen,' he said.

'Friend,' said Pwyll, 'what is your request?'

'The woman I love most – you are sleeping with her tonight.[12] And I have come to ask for her and the provisions and the preparations which are here.'

Pwyll fell silent, for there was no answer which he could have given.

'Be silent as long as you wish,' said Rhiannon. 'Never was a man more feeble in his own wits than you have been.'

'Lady,' he replied, 'I did not know who he was!'

'That is the man to whom it was intended I be given against my will,' she said, 'Gwawl son of Clud, a wealthy man with many followers. But since it has happened that you said what you have said, give me to him, lest there be disgrace to you.'

'Lady,' he said, 'I do not know what kind of answer that is. I could not ever do what you say.'

'You give me to him,' she said, 'and I will make it so that he will never have me.'

'How will that be?' asked Pwyll.

'I will put a small bag in your hand,' she said, 'and keep that with you well. And he asks for the feast and the provisions and the preparations, but that is not in your power. And I will give the feast to the household troops and the retinues,' she said, 'and that will be your answer as to that. In regard to me,' she said, 'I will make

an appointment with him, a year from tonight, to sleep with me. And at the end of the year,' she said, 'you be in the orchard above as one of a hundred knights, and this bag with you. And when he is in the midst of his pleasure and his revelry, you come in yourself, with ragged clothes upon you, and the bag in your hand,' she said, 'and ask for nothing except the fill of the bag with food. I will bring it about,' she said, 'that whatever is placed in it of such food and drink as there is in these seven cantrefs, it will be no more full than before. And after a great deal has been put in it, he will ask you, 'Will your bag ever be full?' You say, 'It will not unless a very wealthy nobleman will rise up and press the food in the bag with his feet and say: Enough has been put in here!' And I will bring it about that he will go to tread down the food in the bag. And when he goes, you twist the bag so that he goes over his head into the bag, and then tie a knot in the strings of the bag. And let there be a good hunting horn around your neck, and when he is tied in the bag, you give a blast on your horn, and let that be as a signal between you and your knights. When they hear the blast of your horn, let them descend upon the court.'

'Lord,' said Gwawl, 'it would be high time for me to get an answer concerning what I asked.'

'As much of what you have asked,' said Pwyll, 'as may be in my power, you shall have it.'

'Friend,' said Rhiannon, 'in regard to the feast and the preparation that is here, I have given that to the men of Dyfed and to the household troops and the retinues that are here. I will not allow that to be given to anyone. A

12 In medieval Welsh, *kyscu gan,* literally 'to sleep with,' also meant 'to marry.'

year from tonight there will be a feast prepared in this court for you, friend, to sleep with me.'

Gwawl journeyed toward his realm. Pwyll came to Dyfed. And each of them spent that year until the time for the feast in the court of Hefeydd the Old. Gwawl son of Clud came to the feast which was prepared for him, and approached the court, and he was welcomed. Pwyll Head of Annwn came to the orchard as one of a hundred knights, as Rhiannon had ordered him, and the bag with him. Pwyll wore heavy rags about himself, and he had great rag boots on his feet. And when he knew that the revelry after the meal had begun, he came to the hall, and after he came to the upper end of the hall, he greeted Gwawl son of Clud and his companions, both men and women.

'May God prosper you,' said Gwawl, 'and God's welcome to you.'

'Lord,' he replied, 'may God repay you. I am on an errand to you.'

'Welcome to your errand,' he said, and if you ask a reasonable request of me, gladly shall you have it.'

'It is reasonable, lord,' he said. 'I ask nothing except out of need. This is the request I ask – the fill of the small bag you see with food.'

'That is a modest request,' he said, 'and you shall have it gladly. Bring food to him,' he said.

A great number of officers rose up and began to fill the bag. But despite what was put into it, it would be no more full than before.

'Friend,' asked Gwawl, will your bag ever be full?'

'It will not, between me and God,' he answered, 'whatever may be put in it, unless

a nobleman of land and earth and wealth rises and treads down the food in the bag with his feet and says, "Enough has been put in here."''

'Ah, champion,' said Rhiannon to Gwawl son of Clud, 'rise up quickly.'

'I will, gladly,' he said, and he rose up and placed his feet in the bag, and Pwyll twisted the bag so that Gwawl would be over his head in the bag, and quickly he closed the bag and tied a knot in the strings, and gave a blast on his horn. And upon that, behold, the household troops about the court, and then they took each of the retinue that came with Gwawl and placed him in his own bonds. And Pwyll threw off the rags and the rag boots and the ragged garb.

And as each one of his retinue would come in, each would strike a single blow to the bag and would ask, 'What is here?'

'A badger,' they would say. This is the kind of game they would play – each one would strike a single blow to the bag either with his foot or with a staff, and thus they played a game with the bag.

Each one as he came would ask, 'What game are you playing thus?'

'The game of badger-in-a-bag,' they would say. And that is when badger-in-a-bag was first played.

'Lord,' said the man from the bag, 'if you will listen to me, it would not be a fit death for me – to kill me in a bag!'

'Lord,' said Hefeydd the Old, 'it is true what he says. It is right for you to listen to him. Not a fit death for him, that.'

'Yea,' replied Pwyll, 'I will take your counsel about him.'

'Here is your counsel,' said Rhiannon then. 'You are in a position appropriate for you to satisfy suppliants and musicians. Let him then give to everyone for you,' she said, 'and take a pledge from him that there will not ever be claim nor revenge for it, and that will be sufficient punishment for him.'

'He will get that gladly,' said the man from the bag.

'And I will take it gladly,' said Pwyll, 'on the counsel of Hefeydd and Rhiannon.'

'That is our counsel,' they said.

'I will take it,' said Pwyll. 'Seek guarantors for you.'

'We will be that for him,' said Hefeydd, 'until his men are free to stand for him.'

And upon that he was released from the bag, and his chief men were freed.

'Now ask guarantors of Gwawl,' said Hefeydd. 'We will recognize those whom it is entitled to take from him.'

Hefeydd listed the guarantors.

'Draw up your conditions yourself,' said Gwawl.

'I am satisfied,' said Pwyll, 'as Rhiannon drew them up.'

The guarantors came on those conditions.

'Yea, lord,' said Gwawl, 'I am bruised and I have taken a great wound – and I have need of a bath – and I will depart, with your permission. But I will leave noblemen here to answer for me all who may make requests of you.'

'Gladly,' said Pwyll, 'do that.'

Gwawl went toward his realm.

The hall, then, was prepared for Pwyll and his retinue, and for the retinue of the court after that, and they went to the tables to sit. And as they had sat a year from that night, everyone sat that night. They engaged in feasting and revelry, and the time came to go to sleep. And Pwyll and Rhiannon went to the chamber, and spent that night in pleasure and contentment.

And the next day, when the day was still young, 'Lord,' said Rhiannon, 'rise up and begin satisfying the musicians, and do not refuse any today who desires a gift.'

'That I will do gladly,' replied Pwyll, 'both today and every day while this feast continues.'

Pwyll rose up and had silence proclaimed to ask all suppliants and musicians to appear, and he told them that each of them would be satisfied according to his will and his whim. And that was done. That feast was spent and no one was refused while it continued.

And when the feast came to an end, 'Lord,' said Pwyll to Hefeydd, 'I will set out, with your permission, toward Dyfed tomorrow.'

'Yea,' replied Hefeydd, 'may God ease the way before you. And make an appointment and a time that Rhiannon may come after you.'

'Between me and God,' declared Pwyll, 'we will set out together from here.'

'Is that what you wish, lord?' asked Hefeydd.

'Yes, between me and God,' said Pwyll.

They set out the next day toward Dyfed, and they made for the court of Arberth, and a feast was prepared for them there. A gathering of the best men and the best women of the land and the realm came to them. No man nor woman of those departed from Rhiannon to whom she did not give a memorable gift, either of a brooch, or of a ring, or of a precious stone.

Preseli. The Preseli Hills stretch across northern Dyfed, as seen here from the prehistoric stone circle at Gors Fawr.

*T*hey ruled the land successfully that year and the next, but in the third year the men of the land began to become heavy of heart at seeing a man whom they loved as much as their lord and their foster-brother without an heir, and they summoned him to them. This is the place they came together – Preseli in Dyfed.

'Lord,' they said, 'we know that you are not as old as some of the men of this land, but our fear is that you will get no heir from the woman who is with you. And because of that, take another woman from whom you may get an heir. You will not last,' they said, 'forever, and though you may love to be thus, we will not suffer it from you.'

'Yea,' answered Pwyll, 'not long yet have we been together, and many an event may happen. Delay this with me until the end of a year. And we will make an appointment to come together a year from this time, and I will abide by your counsel.' They made the appointment.

Before the full time of the meeting came, a son was born to him, and he was born in Arberth. And the night he was born, women were brought to watch the boy and his mother. This is what the women did – they slept, as did the mother of the boy, Rhiannon. This is the number of the women who were brought to the chamber – six women. They watched part of the night, but at that, nevertheless, before midnight each one of them slept, and toward cock-crow awoke. And when they awoke, they looked in the place they had put the boy, but there was nothing of him there.

'Alas,' said one of the women, 'the boy has been lost!'

'Yea,' said another, 'it would be small revenge to burn us or execute us because of the boy.'

'Is there,' said one of the women, 'any counsel in the world in regard to that?'

'Yes,' said another, 'I know good counsel,' she said.

'What is that?' they asked.

'There is a stag-hound bitch here,' she said, 'and she has pups. Let's kill some of the pups, and let's smear Rhiannon's own face with the blood, and her hands, and let's throw the bones across her breast, and let's insist that she herself destroyed the boy. And the insistence of the six of us will not fail against her on her own.' And that counsel was decided upon.

Toward day, Rhiannon awoke and said, 'Ah, women,' she said, 'where is the boy?'

'Lady,' they replied, 'Don't you ask us for the boy! There is not one of us without bruises and blows from struggling with you, and we are without doubt that we have never seen so much strength in one woman as in you, but it did not avail us to struggle with you. You yourself have destroyed your son, and do not demand him from us.'

'Ah, poor things,' said Rhiannon, 'by the Lord God who knows everything, do not accuse me falsely. And if you are afraid, by my confession to God, I will protect you.'

'God knows,' they replied, 'we will not let harm come to ourselves for anyone in the world.'

'Ah, poor things,' she said, 'you will get no harm for speaking the truth.'

Whatever she might say fairly and with pity, she got nothing but the same answer from the women.

Upon that, Pwyll Head of Annwn arose, and the household troop and the retinues, and that misfortune could not be hid. The tale went through the land, and all of the nobles heard it. And the nobles came together to make representations to Pwyll to ask him to divorce his wife for an atrocity as dreadful as what she had done.

This is the answer that Pwyll gave – 'They have no reason to ask me to divorce my wife except that she had no offspring. I know she has had offspring, and I will not divorce her. If she has done wrong, let her receive her punishment for it.'

13 The name Teyrnon derives from an earlier Celtic form *Tigernonos, 'divine king' and can be paired with the name Rhiannon; see note 11 above. His name is preserved in the names of the stream of Nant Teyrnon and the 12th-century abbey of Llantarnam in Gwent. The epithet *Twrf Liant* is somewhat obscure. *Twrf* means 'noise, commotion, tumult'; *Liant* might be from *bliant* 'linen or a similar material' or from *lliant* 'sea, waters, flood'. It has been suggested that the epithet might thus be rendered 'Thunder of Waters' as possibly a reference to the water's noise in the Severn bore; however, by his repeated use of the word *twrf* in this episode, the narrator seems to imply a connection with the May Eve tumult of the tale.

Teyrnon Twrf Liant. Wild garlic flowering beside a stream which may be the Nant Teyrnon, in the grounds of Llantarnam abbey in Gwent. Both names preserve the name of Teyrnon Twrf Liant.

Rhiannon herself summoned scholars and wise men to her, and after it seemed better to her to take her punishment than to quarrel with the women, she took her punishment. This is the punishment that was put upon her – to be in that court in Arberth until the end of seven years – and there was a mounting block beside the gate – to sit beside that every day, and to tell to all who might come, whom she supposed might not know it, that whole tale; and whoever might allow her to carry him, to offer to carry guest and stranger upon her back to the court. But rarely would anyone allow her to carry him. And thus she spent part of the year.

And at that time Teyrnon Twrf Liant was lord over Gwent Is Coed, and he was the best man in the world.[13] And in his household there was a mare, and there was neither horse nor mare fairer than she in the kingdom. And each May Eve she would give birth, but no one could find out a single word about her foal. This is what Teyrnon did – he conversed one night with his wife.

'Ah, wife,' he said, 'We have been neglectful every year to allow offspring to the mare without keeping a single one of them.'

'What can be done about that?' she said.

'God's revenge on me,' he said, '– tonight is May Eve – if I do not find out what fate is taking the foals.'

He had the mare brought indoors, and he put on his arms, and began the night watch. And as night began, the mare gave birth to a fine great foal, and it stood right on the spot.

This is what Teyrnon did – he rose up and looked on the sturdiness of the foal. And as he was thus, he could hear a great tumult, and after the tumult, behold, a great claw coming through the window of the house and seizing the foal by its mane. This is what Teyrnon did – he drew his sword and cut off the arm at the elbow, so that that much of the arm and the foal remained with him inside. And upon that he heard a tumult and a shriek both together. He opened the door and rushed after the tumult. He could not see the tumult because the night was so dark. He rushed after it and followed it. But he remembered leaving the door open, and he returned. And by the door, behold, a small boy in swaddling-clothes, wrapped in a cloak of silk brocade. He took up the boy, and behold, the boy was strong for the age that was upon him.

He barred the door and went to the chamber where his wife was.

'Lady,' he said, 'are you sleeping?'

'No, lord,' she answered. 'I was sleeping, but when you came in, I woke up.'

'Here is a son for you,' he said, 'if you wish, that which you have never had.'

'Lord,' she asked, 'what tale is that?'

'Here it all is –,' said Teyrnon, and he related the whole account.

'Yea, lord,' she asked, 'what sort of garment is about the boy?'

'A cloak of silk brocade,' he said.

'He is the son of gentlefolk,' she said. 'Lord,' she said, 'a joy and a comfort would be to me – if you wished it – that I would bring women into league with me, and we would say that I am pregnant.'

'I myself agree with you, gladly,' he said, 'about that.' And thus was it done. They had the boy baptized according to the baptism that was done then. This is the name that was given to him – Gwri Golden Hair. What there was of hair on his head was as yellow as gold.

The boy was nurtured in the court until he was a year old. And before he was a year old he was walking steadily, and he was stronger than a three-year-old boy who was large in growth and size. And a second year he was nurtured and he was as strong as a six-year-old boy. And before the end of the fourth year he was bargaining with the grooms of the horses to let him lead them to water.

'Lord,' said his wife to Teyrnon, 'where is the foal you saved the night you got the boy?'

'I entrusted it to the grooms of the horses, and I asked that it be looked after.'

'Would it not please you, lord,' she asked, 'to have it broken in and given to the boy? For the night you got the boy, the foal was born and you saved it.'

'I will not go against that,' replied Teyrnon. 'I will let you give it to him.'

'Lord,' she said, 'God repay you. I will give it to him.'

The horse was given to the boy, and she came to the stablemen and to the grooms of the horses to command them to look after the horse, and that it be broken in by the time the boy might learn his horsemanship – and there is a tale about that.

Meanwhile, they heard news concerning Rhiannon, and about her punishment. This is what Teyrnon Twrf Liant did, because of the prize he had got – he listened to the tale and asked continually about it, until he heard from many of the multitude who had come to the court increasing complaints about the sadness of Rhiannon's misfortune and her punishment. This is what Teyrnon himself did – he thought about that, and he looked closely at the boy, and it came into his mind that as regards appearance he had never seen a son and a father as alike as the boy to Pwyll Head of Annwn. Pwyll's form was familiar to him, because he had been a man of his before that. And after that grief took hold of him, because of how wrong it was for him to keep the boy with him when he knew he was the son of another man. And as soon as he got some privacy with his wife, he told her that it was not right for them to keep the boy with them, and to allow a punishment as great as there was on a noblewoman as good as Rhiannon for that reason, and the boy a son to Pwyll Head of Annwn.

And she, Teyrnon's wife, agreed on sending the boy to Pwyll. 'And three things, Lord,' she said, 'shall we get from that: thanks and bounty for releasing Rhiannon from the punishment she is in, and thanks from Pwyll for nurturing the boy and restoring him to him, and the third thing, if the boy becomes a kindly man, he will be a foster son to us, and the best that he might ever do, he will do for us.'

And they decided on that counsel. And it was no later for them than the next day that Teyrnon equipped himself as one of three knights, and the boy as a fourth with them, on the horse which Teyrnon had given him. And they made their way toward Arberth.

It was not long before they came to Arberth. As they approached the court, they could see Rhiannon sitting beside the mounting block. As they came up to her, 'Ah, chieftain,' she said, 'go no farther than that. I will carry each one of you to the court. And that is my penance, for killing my own son myself and destroying him.'

'Ah, gentlelady,' said Teyrnon, 'I do not imagine that any one of us will go upon your back.'

'Let him go who wishes it,' said the boy, 'I shall not!'

'God knows, friend,' said Teyrnon, 'we shall not!'

They approached the court, and they were met with great joy. And they had begun to hold a feast at the court. Pwyll himself had come from a circuit of Dyfed. They went into the hall and to wash. And Pwyll welcomed Teyrnon, and they went to sit. This is how they sat – Teyrnon between Pwyll and Rhiannon, and Teyrnon's two companions above Pwyll, with the boy between them.

After finishing eating and beginning the revelry, they conversed. This was Teyrnon's conversation – he related the whole adventure of the mare and of the boy, and how the boy had been under their care, Teyrnon and his wife, and they raised him.

'And behold there your son, lady,' said Teyrnon, 'and whoever spoke a lie against you did wrong. And when I myself heard the care that was upon you, I was sorry and I grieved. And I do not imagine there is anyone in this whole company who does not recognize that the boy is the son of Pwyll,' said Teyrnon.

Ystrad Tywi.
Looking south-east
across Ystrad Tywi
near the border
of Ceredigion.

'There is no one,' they all said, 'who wouldn't be certain of that.'

'Between me and God,' said Rhiannon, 'it would deliver me from my care if that were true.'

'Lady,' said Pendaran Dyfed, 'you have named your son well – Pryderi – and that suits him best – Pryderi son of Pwyll Head of Annwn.'

'See,' said Rhiannon, 'if his own name might not suit him best.'

'What is the name?' asked Pendaran Dyfed.

'Gwri Golden Hair is the name we gave him.'

'Pryderi,' said Pendaran Dyfed, 'will be his name.'

'That is more fitting,' said Pwyll, '– taking a name for the boy from the word his mother spoke when she had joyful news about him.' And that was settled on.[14]

'Teyrnon,' said Pwyll, 'God repay you for raising this boy until now. And it is right for him, if he will be a kindly man, to repay you.'

'Lord,' replied Teyrnon, 'the woman who raised him – there is not anyone in the world with more grief than she after losing him. It is right for him to remember, for me and for that woman, what we have done for him.'

'Between me and God,' declared Pwyll,

[14] The narrator derives the name Pryderi from Rhiannon's statement, *oed escor uym pryder im*, 'it would deliver me from my care,' or more literally 'it would be a deliverance of my care from me,' perhaps with a play on *escor* in the sense of 'delivery, birth.' *Pryder* means 'care, anxiety, concern, fear.' Ifor Williams

Ceredigion. The Teifi Pools, in the hills of eastern Ceredigion, above Strata Florida, are the source of the river Teifi.

suggests that an earlier text may have read *pryderi* 'loss' (compare the Old Breton form *pritiri* which glosses the Latin *iactura* 'loss, sacrifice'), rather than the *pryder* of the White and Red Book manuscripts.

'while I live I will maintain you, both you and your realm, as long as I can maintain my own. If he lives, it is better for him to maintain you than for me. And if that is your counsel, and that of these noblemen, since you have raised him until now, we will give him to Pendaran Dyfed to foster from now on. And you will be companions and foster-fathers to him.'

'That,' they all said, 'is proper counsel.'

And then the boy was given to Pendaran Dyfed, and the noblemen of the land joined with him. And Teyrnon Twrf Liant and his companions set out for his land and his realm with love and gladness. And he did not go without being offered the fairest jewels and the best horses and the most prized hounds. But he did not wish for anything.

Then they remained in their realm, and Pryderi son of Pwyll Head of Annwn was raised carefully, as was proper, until he was the most perfect lad, and the fairest, and the most accomplished in every noble feat of anyone in the realm.[15] Thus they spent years and years, until an end came to the life of Pwyll Head of Annwn and he died. And then Pryderi ruled the seven cantrefs of Dyfed prosperously, loved by his realm and by all around him. And after that he conquered the three cantrefs of Ystrad Tywi, and the four cantrefs of Ceredigion, and those were called the seven cantrefs of Seisyllwch. And Pryderi son of Pwyll Head of Annwn was at that conquest until it came into his mind to marry. This is the wife he desired – Cigfa daughter of Gwyn Gohoyw son of Gloyw Wallt Lydan son of Casnar Wledig, of the nobles of this island.

and thus ends this branch of THE MABINOGI

[15] In his Welsh dictionary published in 1632, John Davies prints a list of the *Twenty-Four Noble Feats*. These include *Ten Manly Feats*: 6 bodily feats (Strength, Running, Jumping, Swimming, Wrestling, Riding), and 4 feats of arms (Archery, Fencing with sword and buckler, Fencing with a two-handed sword, Fencing with a quarterstaff); *Ten Youthful Feats*: 3 for hunting (Hunting with hounds, Hunting fish, Hunting birds) and 7 Domestic Feats (Poetry, Playing the harp, Reading Welsh, Singing a *cywydd* [a type of poem] to harp accompaniment, Singing a four-line *cywydd*, and accenting it, Drawing Arms, Heraldry); and *Four Minor Feats:* Playing *gwyddbwyll* [a chess-like board game], Playing *tawlbwrdd* [another board game with an unequal number of pieces on each side], Playing dice, Tuning a harp. This list, though later than *The Mabinogi*, gives an idea of the sorts of accomplishments expected of a young Welsh nobleman in the Middle Ages.

Dyfed sunset.
Sunset over Dinas
Head on the coast
of northern Dyfed.

126

127

Harddlech (Harlech). The rock of Harlech, where the famous castle built by Edward I now stands in ruin, commands a view far out over Cardigan Bay and the Irish Sea.

here is the second branch of

THE MABINOGI

BENDIGEIDFRAN son of Llŷr was crowned king over this island and adorned with the crown of London.[16] And one afternoon he was in Harddlech, in Ardudwy, in a court of his.[17] And they were sitting on the rock of Harddlech, above the sea, and Manawydan son of Llŷr with him, and two brothers of the same mother as he – Nisien and Efnisien, and nobles beside those, as would be fitting around a king. The two

Ardudwy. Old walls leading down to Llyn Irddyn in Ardudwy.

brothers of the same mother as he were sons of Euroswydd by his mother Penarddun daughter of Beli son of Mynogan.[18] And one of those lads was a good lad – he could bring about peace between two hosts when they would be most wrathful. That was Nisien. The other could cause strife between two brothers when they loved one another the most.

And as they were sitting thus, they could see thirteen ships coming from the south of Ireland and making way toward them, with a swift, easy motion, the wind at their back, and swiftly drawing near to them.

'I see ships yonder,' said the king, 'and coming boldly toward the land. And ask men of the court to array themselves and go to see what is their intention.'

The men arrayed themselves and approached them below. After seeing the ships from nearby, they were certain they had never seen ships better fitted than they. On them were fair banners of brocaded silk, seemly and brave.

And upon that, behold, one of the ships outstripping the others, and they could see a shield raised above the gunwale of the ship, with the point of the shield upward as a sign of peace. And the men drew near to them, so they could hear one another's conversation. They put out boats and approached the land and greeted the king. The king could hear them from where he was on the rock high above their heads.

'May God reward you,' he said, 'and welcome to you. Whose is this fleet of ships, and who is chief over them?'

'Lord,' they said, 'here is Matholwch, king of Ireland, and the ships are his.'

[18] A tale of antagonism between the two husbands of Penarddun is hinted at in the triad of the 'Three Exalted Prisoners of the Island of Britain,' the first of whom is 'Llŷr Half-Speech, who was imprisoned by Euroswydd;' Rachel Bromwich, *Trioedd Ynys Prydein: The Welsh Triads*, number 52.

[19] The triad of the Three Chief Forebears (*rieni*) does not appear in any of the surviving texts of triads, unless that of the Three Great Queens (*rhiein*) of Arthur, all of whom are named Gwenhwyfar (= Guinevere), is a late version of a Three Great Queens triad that originally included Branwen. Some have suggested that the other two should then be Rhiannon and Aranrhod, from the first and fourth branches, but this is highly speculative; see Bromwich, *Trioedd*, lxxxvii.

[20] Aberffraw, in Anglesey, was traditionally the chief court of the kings of Gwynedd in North Wales.

Aberffraw. The chief court of the medieval rulers of Gwynedd was located where old stone cottages now stand near the mouth (*aber*) of the river Ffraw.

'What,' said the king, 'might he desire? Does he desire to come to land?'

'He does not, lord,' they said, ' – he is engaged on an errand to you – unless he gets his errand.'

'What sort of errand is his?' said the king.

'Wishing to ally himself with you, lord,' they said. 'He came to ask for Branwen daughter of Llŷr. And if it pleases you, he wishes to bind the Island of the Mighty and Ireland together, so they would be stronger.'

'Yea,' he said, 'let them come to land, and we will take counsel about that.'

That answer went to him. 'I will go gladly,' he said. He came to land and they welcomed him. And there was a great gathering in the court that night, between his retinue and the retinue of the court.

Straightway the next day they took counsel. This is what was arrived at in the council – to give Branwen to Matholwch. And she was one of the Three Chief Forebears of this island.[19] The fairest maiden in the world was she. And a time was appointed in Aberffraw to sleep with her, and thence they set out.[20] And those retinues set out toward Aberffraw – Matholwch and his retinues in the ships, Bendigeidfran and his retinue on land – until they came as far as Aberffraw.

In Aberffraw the feast and the sitting

began. This is how they sat – the king of the Island of the Mighty, with Manawydan son of Llŷr on one side of him and Matholwch on the other side, and Branwen daughter of Llŷr with him.

They were not within a house, but in tents. Bendigeidfran had never been contained within a house.

And they began the revelry. They pursued the revelry and conversation, and when they saw that it was better for them to take sleep than to continue the revelry, they went to sleep. And that night Matholwch slept with Branwen.

And the next day each of the retinue of the court arose, and the officers began to discuss the billeting of the horses and the servants. And they billeted them in every part as far as the sea.

And upon that one day, behold, Efnisien, the quarrelsome man we mentioned above, happened upon the quarters of Matholwch's horses, and he asked whose were the horses.

'These are the horses of Matholwch King of Ireland,' they said.

'What are they doing here?' he said.

'The king of Ireland is here, and he has slept with Branwen, your sister, and these are his horses.'

'Is it thus they have done with a maiden as good as that – and a sister to me – to give her without my permission? They could not do a greater insult to me,' he said. And upon that he pushed in among the horses and cut the lips to their teeth, and the ears to the heads, and the hair to the back, and where he could get a grip on the eyelids, he cut them to the bone. And he disfigured the horses thus, until there was no use that could be made of the horses.

The tale came to Matholwch. This is how it came – he was told of the disfiguring of his horses and their spoiling, until there wasn't a single use that could be made of them.

'Yea, lord,' said one, 'disgrace has been done to you, and it was intended to do that to you.'

'God knows, it is strange to me – if they wished to disgrace me – to give a maiden so good, of such rank, so beloved by her kindred, as they have given to me.'

'Lord,' said another, 'you see it made plain. And there is nothing you may do except make for your ships.'

And upon that he sought his ships.

The tale came to Bendigeidfran that Matholwch was leaving the court, without asking, without permission. And messengers went to ask him why that was. These are the messengers who went – Iddig son of Anarawd,[21] and Hefeydd the Tall. Those men overtook him and they asked him what was his intention, and for what reason was he going away.

'God knows,' he said, 'if I had known that, I would not have come here. Total disgrace I have received, and no one has taken a worse journey than I have taken here. And a strange thing has happened to me.'

'What is that?' they said.

'Giving me Branwen daughter of Llŷr, one of the Three Chief Forebears of this island, and daughter to a king of the Island of the Mighty, and my sleeping with her, and after that disgracing me. And it was strange to me, that the disgrace that was to be done to me was not done before giving a maiden as good as that to me.'

21 The manuscript reading *Anarawc* is probably a scribal error for *Anarawt* (*Anarawd* in modern Welsh spelling).

22 The medieval Welsh spelling is ambiguous; Unic Glew Yscwyd could represent, in Modern Welsh spelling, either Unig Glew Ysgwydd 'U. Stout (or Brave) Shoulder' or Unig Glew Ysgwyd 'U. Stout Shield.'

[23] The phrase *a'e uys bychan*, not found in the manusripts, was suggested by Ifor Williams on the basis of close parallels with medieval Welsh law texts. 'The insult-price of the King of Aberffraw is paid thus: a hundred cows for every cantref he has, with a red-eared bull for every hundred cows, and a rod of gold [*some texts say silver*] as tall as himself and as thick as his little finger, and a plate of gold as broad as his face and as thick as the nail of a plough-man who has been a ploughman for seven years. Gold is not paid save to the King of Aberffraw.' Dafydd Jenkins, *The Law of Hywel Dda*, p. 5-6.

[24] A commot [from Welsh *cwmwd*] is a division of a cantref; see note 2. The name, Talebolion, probably derives from *tal* 'end' + *y* '(of) the' + *bolion*, plural of *bôl* 'belly', '(rounded) hill' or 'valley.' However, the storyteller understands it as *tal* 'payment' + *ebolion* '(of) foals.'

'God knows, lord, not by the will of the one who owns the court,' they said, 'nor any of his council was that disgrace done to you. And though that may be a disgrace to you, greater it is to Bendigeidfran than to you, that insult and that trick.'

'Yea,' he said, 'I suppose. But nevertheless he cannot undo my disgrace because of that.'

Those men returned with that answer toward the place where Bendigeidfran was and told him the answer Matholwch had spoken.

'Yea,' he said, 'his leaving angrily is no relief, and we will not allow it.'

'Yea, lord,' they said, 'send messengers after him again.'

'I will,' he replied. 'Rise up Manawydan son of Llŷr, and Hefeydd the Tall, and Unig Stout Shoulder[22] and go after him,' he said, 'and tell him he shall get a healthy horse for each one that was damaged, and along with that he shall get as his honour-price a silver staff that will be as thick as his little finger and as tall as he himself, and a gold plate as broad as his face.[23] And tell him what kind of man did that, and that it is against my own will that that was done, and that it is a brother with the same mother as I who did that, and it is not easy for me either to kill him or to destroy him. But let him come to visit with me,' he said, 'and I will make peace in the form he himself might wish.'

The messengers went after Matholwch, and they related to him that speech in a friendly way, and he heard it.

'Ah, men,' he said, 'we will take counsel.'

He went into his council. This is the counsel they thought of – if they refused that, it would be more likely for them to get greater shame than to get greater compensation, and they decided on taking that.

And they came to the court peacefully. And they prepared tents and pavilions for them similar to the preparations of a hall, and they went to eat. And as they had begun sitting at the beginning of the feast, they sat then.

And Matholwch and Bendigeidfran began to converse. And behold, the conversation that he had from Matholwch seemed listless to Bendigeidfran, and sad, and his joy had been constant before that. And he thought that the chieftain was sorrowful because of the smallness of the reparation for his injury.

'Ah, man,' said Bendigeidfran, 'you are not as good a conversationalist tonight as the other night. And if it is that your reparation seems so small to you, you shall get it added to according to your wish, and tomorrow your horses will be repaid to you.'

'Lord,' he replied, 'May God repay you.'

'I will also enhance your reparation for you,' said Bendigeidfran. 'I will give you a cauldron, and the remarkable characteristic of the cauldron is this – a man of yours who may be killed today, cast him in the cauldron, and by tomorrow he will be as good as he was at his best, except that he will not have the power of speech.'

And he thanked him for that, and he took great joy because of that. And the next day his horses were repaid to him, while trained horses lasted. And then he was taken to another commot, and foals were repaid to him, until the payment to him was complete. And because of that, the name Talebolion was given to that commot from then on.[24]

Talebolion.
The low
rounded ridges
of Talebolion
in northwest
Anglesey, seen
from Gorsedd
y Penrhyn on
Ynys Gybi
(Holy Island).

And the second night they sat together. 'Lord,' said Matholwch, 'where did the cauldron come from that you gave to me?'

'It came to me,' he answered, 'from a man who was from your land, and I don't know that he didn't get it there.'

'Who was that?' he asked.

'Llassar Llaes Gyfnewid,' he replied. 'And he came here from Ireland, and Cymidei Cymeinfoll, his wife, with him. And they escaped from the iron house in Ireland when it was made white-hot around them, and they escaped from there. And it is strange to me if you do not know anything about that.'

'I do, lord,' he said, 'and as much as I know, I will relate to you. I was hunting in Ireland one day on top of a mound above a lake there was in Ireland, and it was called the Lake of the Cauldron. And I could see a large red-haired man coming from the lake with a cauldron on his back. And he was also a great monstrous man, with an evil, ugly look about him – and a woman behind him. And if he was big, his wife was more than twice as big as he. And they came toward me and greeted me.

"Yea,' I said, 'what journey are you on?'

"Here is the journey we are on, lord,' he said, ' – this woman,' he said, 'at the end of a fortnight and a month will become pregnant, and the boy that will be born then of that bellyful, at the end of a fortnight and a month, will be a fully armed fighting man.'

'I took them to me, to make provision for them. They were with me for a year. During the year I kept them without resentment; from then on, they were resented by me. And before the end of the fourth month they themselves were making themselves hated and unbearable in the land, committing outrages and molesting and harassing noblemen and noblewomen. From then on, my realm rose up about me to ask me to separate from them, and to give a choice to me, either my realm or them.

'I put it to the council of my land what could be done about them. They would not go of their own will; there was no need for them to go against their will, because of their ability to fight. And then in that quandary they decided to make a chamber completely of iron, and after the chamber was ready, summoned what there was of smiths in Ireland then, of those who owned tongs and hammer, and had coal piled as high as the roof-ridge of the chamber, and had food and drink served unstintingly to them – to the woman, and her husband, and her children. And when it was known that they were drunk, they began mixing fire with the coal upon the chamber, and blowing the bellows that had been set around the house, with a man for each two bellows, and they began to blow the bellows until the house was completely white-hot about their heads. And then they held a council in the middle of the floor of the chamber. And he waited until the wall was white-hot, and in spite of the very great heat, he charged the wall with his shoulder and knocked it out, and after him his wife. But none escaped from there except him and his wife. And then, as I suppose, lord,' said Matholwch to Bendigeidfran, 'he came across to you.'

'Then, God knows,' he said, 'he came here, and he gave the cauldron to me.'

'How, lord, did you receive them?'

'By quartering them everywhere in the realm, and they are numerous and rising up everywhere and growing strong wherever they may be, in men and arms, the best anyone has seen.'

They pursued the conversation that night as long as it pleased them, and song and revelry. And when they saw that it would be better for them to go to sleep than to sit any longer, to sleep they went. And thus they spent that feast in pleasure. And at the end of that, Matholwch set out, and Branwen with him, toward Ireland. And thereupon thirteen ships set out from Abermenai and they came to Ireland.

Abermenai. Looking west through the mouth (*aber*) of the Menai Strait.

Caer Saint yn Arfon. The foundations of the Roman fort of Segontium at Caernarfon on the river Seiont or Saint.

[25] In the triad of 'Three Harmful Blows of the Island of Britain', Matholwch himself strikes the blow: 'The first of them Matholwch the Irishman struck upon Branwen daughter of Llŷr; The second Gwenhwyfach struck upon Gwenhwyfar [= Guinevere]: and for that cause there took place afterwards the Action of the Battle of Camlan; And the third Golydan the Poet struck upon Cadwaladr the Blessed'; Bromwich, *Trioedd*, number 53.

In Ireland they were received with very great joy. No great man nor noblewoman came to see Branwen to whom she did not give either a clasp or a ring or a treasured royal jewel that it would be remarkable to see given away. And amongst all that, she gained great honour that year, and she prospered in honour and companions. And in the meantime, it happened that she became pregnant, and after the proper time passed, a son was born to her. This is the name that was given to the boy – Gwern son of Matholwch. The boy was placed in fosterage in the best place for men in Ireland.

And thereupon, in the second year, behold, a murmuring in Ireland about the disgrace Matholwch had received in Wales, and the shameful trick that had been done to him over his horses. And thereupon his foster brother and the men closest to him taunting him with that, and without hiding it. And, lo, a rising in Ireland so that there was no peace for him unless he got revenge for the insult. This is the revenge they decided on – to drive Branwen from the same chamber as he, and compel her to cook in the court, and have the butcher, after he had been cutting meat, come to her and box her on the ear every day. And thus was her punishment carried out.[25]

'Yea, lord,' said his men to Matholwch, 'now make a ban on all ships and boats and coracles, so that no one may go to Wales, and whoever may come here from Wales, imprison them and do not let them go back, lest this become known.' And they decided on that.

They were thus for no less than three years.

And in the meantime, she nurtured a starling on the end of the kneading-trough with her, and taught speech to it, and told the bird the kind of man her brother was. And she brought a letter about the punishment and the dishonour that was upon her, and the letter was bound at the base of the bird's wings, and she sent it toward Wales, and the bird came to this island.

This is where it found Bendigeidfran – in Caer Saint in Arfon, in an assembly of his one day.[26] And landing on his shoulder, it ruffled its feathers so that the letter was caught sight of, and he could tell that the bird had been nurtured in an inhabited place. And then he took the letter and looked at it. And when the letter was read, he grew sad at hearing of the punishment that was upon Branwen, and he began on the spot to have messengers sent to muster this entire island. And then he had the complete levy of seven score and fourteen districts come to him, and he himself complained to them of the punishment which was upon his sister. And then he took counsel. This is the counsel that was decided – to make for Ireland and leave seven men as leaders here, with Cradawg son of Brân as chief, and as seven knights. Those men were left in Edeirnon, and because of that the name Saith Marchog was given to the town.[27] These were the seven men – Cradawg son of Brân, and

[26] Caer Saint in Arfon = 'The Fortress on the Saint in (the region) opposite Môn/Anglesey.' The name derives from that of the River Saint or Seiont and the 4th-century Roman fort of Segontium, on the hill just south-east of the 13th-century castle and town, which is now generally called simply Caernarfon. The river flows into the Menai Strait beside the castle. The *dadlau* 'assembly, meeting' was a meeting to hear legal cases, from *dadl* 'debate, argument.'

[27] Saith Marchog = 'Seven Riders,' or 'Seven Knights.' Bryn Saith Marchog is a village in Denbighshire between Rhuthun and Corwen.

Saith Marchog. The village of Bryn Saith Marchog in Edeirnon.

[28] For *Anarawd*, see note 21. Note that the form of the name Llassar Llaes Gyngwyd is different here from that given earlier, Llassar Llaes Gyfnewid, and the variant in the Third Branch, Llassar Llaes Gygnwyd. There is an apparent anachronism in this list; Pendaran Dyfed is named as Pryderi's foster father in the First Branch, yet he appears here as a young lad.

[29] 'Three Chief Officers (or Stewards) of the Island of Britain: Caradawg son of Brân, and Cawrdaf son of Caradawg, and Owain son of Maxen Wledig;' Bromwich, *Trioedd*, number 13. This triad seems to refer to three sons whose fathers led armies from Britain never to return alive. The triad itself is referred to in a (10th or 11th century?) poem in the *Book of Taliesin*: 'Who are the Three Chief Officers who guarded the land?'

Hefeydd the Tall, and Unig Stout Shoulder, and Iddig son of Anarawd Round-hair, and Ffodor son of Erfyll, and Wlch Bone-lip, and Llashar son of Llassar Llaes Gyngwyd, with Pendaran Dyfed as a young lad together with them.[28] Those seven remained as seven stewards to look after this island, with Cradawg as head steward over them.[29]

Bendigeidfran and the host we mentioned sailed toward Ireland. And the sea was not great then; he went by wading. There was nothing but two rivers, called Lli and Archan. And after that the sea increased, when the sea overran the kingdoms. But then he walked, with what there was of stringed minstrelsy on his own back, and made for the land of Ireland.

And Matholwch's swineherds were on the shore of the sea one day, minding their swine. And because of the sight they saw on the sea, they came to Matholwch.

'Lord,' they said, 'greetings to you.'

'May God reward you,' he replied. 'Do you have news?'

'Lord,' they said, 'we have strange news. We saw a wood on the sea, where we have never seen a single tree.'

'There's a strange thing,' he said. 'Did you see anything besides that?'

'We did, lord,' they answered, 'a great mountain close by the wood, and that was on the move, with a lofty ridge on the mountain, and a lake on each side of the ridge, and the wood and the mountain and all of those things on the move.'

'Yea,' he said, 'there is no one here who might know anything about that, unless Branwen knows. Ask her.'

Messengers went to Branwen.

'Lady,' they asked, 'what do you suppose that is?'

'Though I may not be a lady,' she answered, 'I know what that is – the men of the Island of the Mighty coming across, from hearing of my punishment and my dishonour.'

'What is the wood that was seen on the sea?' they asked.

'Alderwood masts and sailyards of ships,' she replied.

'Alas!' they cried. 'What was the mountain that could be seen beside the ships?'

'That,' she said, 'was Bendigeidfran, my brother, coming by wading. There was never a ship which could contain him.'

'What was the lofty ridge with the lake on each side of the ridge?'

'He,' she said, 'looking on this island; he is wrathful. The two lakes on each side of the ridge are his two eyes on each side of his nose.'

And then all the fighting men of Ireland and all the coastlands were quickly mustered, and counsel was taken.

'Lord,' said his noblemen to Matholwch, 'there is no counsel except to retreat across the Llinon – a river that was in Ireland[30] – and leave the river between you and him, and destroy the bridge that is over the river. And there are sucking stones[31] in the bottom of the river; no

ship or vessel can be on it.' They retreated across the river and they destroyed the bridge.

Bendigeidfran came to the land, and the fleet with him, toward the bank of the river.

'Lord,' said his noblemen, 'you know the peculiarity of the river – none can go through it; there is no bridge over it either. What is your counsel about a bridge?' they said.

'There is none,' he replied, 'except "Whoever may be chief, let him be a bridge." I will be a bridge,' he said. And that saying was first spoken then, and it is still used as a proverb.[32]

And then, after he lay across the river, hurdles were cast over him, and his hosts went across over him.[33]

Upon that, as soon as he arose, behold, messengers of Matholwch coming toward him and saluting him, and greeting him from Matholwch, his kinsman, and saying it was his will that nothing but good would come to him.

'And Matholwch is giving the kingship of Ireland to Gwern son of Matholwch, your nephew, your sister's son, and investing him in your presence, in payment for the wrong and the insult that was done to Branwen. And you make provision for Matholwch in whatever place you wish, either here or in the Island of the Mighty.'

'Yea,' said Bendigeidfran, 'if I cannot obtain the kingship myself, perhaps I will take counsel about your message. For now, until a different offer comes, you will get no answer from me.'

'Yea,' they replied, 'the best answer we may get, we will bring to you, and you wait for our message.'

'I will,' he said, 'if you come quickly.'

[30] *Llinon* is the Welsh equivalent of *Sinann*, the Irish name of the river Shannon. However, the incident of the hurdles which follows seems to explain the name of Dublin, which is on the river Liffy; see note 33; thus the manuscript *Llinon* may be an error for *Lliuon*, when -*u*- represents the sound |v|.

[31] i.e. lodestones.

[32] This saying is recorded independently in a collection of proverbs in a 13th-century manuscript of Welsh laws; J. G. Evans, *Facsimile of the Chirk Codex of the Welsh Laws*, 32.25.

[33] A hurdle is a rectangular frame of woven withes. This incident accounts for the Irish name of Dublin, *Baile Átha Cliath* 'the Town of the Ford of the Hurdles.'

The messengers set out, and they came to Matholwch.

'Lord,' they said, 'prepare an answer that might be better for Bendigeidfran. He would not listen to any of the answer we took to him.'

'Ah, men,' said Matholwch, 'what is your counsel?'

'Lord,' they replied, 'there is no counsel for you except one: he has never been contained in a house,' they said. 'Make a house,' they said, 'in his honour, to hold him and the men of the Island of the Mighty in one side of the house, and you and your host in the other side. And give your kingship into his will, and do homage to him. And from the honour of making the house,' they said, ' – a thing he has never had – a house that could hold him – he will make peace with you.'

And the messengers came, and that message with them, to Bendigeidfran, and he took counsel. This is what he decided in his council – to accept that. And all that was through the counsel of Branwen, and that was done by her lest the country be destroyed.

The peace was arranged and the house was built, large and grand. But the Irish planned a trick. This is the trick they planned – to put a peg on each side of each of the one hundred columns there were in the house, and to put a leather bag on each peg, with an armed man in each one of them. This is what Efnisien did – he came in before the host of the Island of the Mighty, and he cast fierce, merciless looks throughout the house. And he perceived the leather bags along the posts.

'What is in this bag?' he asked of one of the Irish.

'Flour, friend,' he replied.

This is what he did – he felt it until he got the head, and he squeezed the head until he felt his fingers sinking into the brain through the bone. And he left that, and he placed his hand on another one and asked, 'What is here?'

'Flour,' replied the Irishman.

This is what he would do – the same game with each one of them, until he had not left a man alive of all the two hundred men except one.

And he came to that one and asked, 'What is here?'

'Flour, friend,' replied the Irishman.

This is what he did – he felt it until he got the head, and as he had squeezed the heads of those others, he squeezed that head. This is what he could feel – the armour on that head. He did not leave that one until he killed him. And then he sang an *englyn*:[34]

There is in this bag a variety of flour,
Champions, warriors, attackers in battle,
Against battlers, battle-ready.

And upon that the retinues came into the house. And the men of Ireland came into the house on one side, and the men of the Island of the Mighty on the other side. And as soon as they sat, there was accord between them, and the boy was invested with the kingship.

And then, after peace was established, Bendigeidfran called the boy to him. From Bendigeidfran, the boy went toward Manawydan, and all of those who saw him, loved him. From

---

[34] An *englyn* is a form of epigrammatic verse, usually of three or four lines. There may be a pun on 'flour,' for in Middle Welsh, *blawd* could also mean 'flower, bloom,' just as English *flour* and *flower* are two spellings of a single original word. The pun, then, suggests 'the flower or best (of warriors).'

[35] The name Morddwyd Tyllion may mean 'Pierced Thigh.' The Welsh syntax here suggests that this line may be taken from an older poem. In a poem in the *Book of Taliesin* we find these lines:
'I was with Brân in Ireland;
I saw when the Morddwyd Tyllon was slain.'
It has been suggested that 'the Pierced Thigh' may refer to Bendigeidfran, and parallels have been drawn between him and Bron, the Fisher King in French Grail legends who had a wound in the thigh or groin.

[36] This is an early reference to the tradition or belief that the Irish fought unclothed. Other examples are known from the 12th century and later; see MacCana, *Branwen*, 116.

[37] *Eil*, literally 'second', here means 'son, grandson, descendant, heir (of)'; compare

Dylan eil Ton in the Fourth Branch.

[38] Taliesin was a 6th-century poet, about a dozen of whose poems have survived in the 14th-century manuscript known as the *Book of Taliesin*, which also attributes to him many later poems dealing with mythological and legendary material, some of which is related to *The Mabinogi*. According to this poetry and to later tales about him, Taliesin gained full knowledge of the past, present, and future; see Patrick K. Ford, *Ystoria Taliesin* (1992).

[39] Since the early 17th century, Gwales has been identified as the small uninhabited island of Grassholm, now home to more than 32,000 pairs of gannets, some seven miles west of Skomer Island off the south-western coast of Dyfed. This island, however, is neither in nor directly off the coast of the medieval cantref of Penfro; thus some other place in Penfro, now lost to us, may be meant. Penfro is usually rendered in English as Pembroke, which was adopted by the Normans and English as the name of the castle, town, and the larger administrative county of Pembrokeshire.

Manawydan, Nisien son of Euroswydd called the boy to him. The boy went to him courteously.

'Why,' said Efnisien, 'does not my nephew, my sister's son, come to me? Even though he were not king of Ireland, I would be pleased to be kindly toward the boy.'

'Let him go, gladly,' said Bendigeidfran.

The boy went to him gladly.

'To God I make my confession,' he thought to himself, 'to this household, what I shall do now is an unimaginable crime to commit.' And rising up, he took the boy by the feet, without delay, and no man in the house got hold of him until he thrust the boy headlong into the blazing fire.

And when Branwen saw her son burning in the fire, she tried to leap into the fire from the place where she was sitting between her two brothers, but Bendigeidfran took her in one hand and his shield in the other. And then everyone rose up throughout the house. And there was the greatest uproar there ever was among a host in a single house, each one taking up his arms.

And then Morddwyd Tyllion said, 'Dogs of Gwern, beware of Morddwyd Tyllion.'[35]

And as everyone went for his arms, Bendigeidfran supported Branwen between his shield and his shoulder.

And then the Irish began to kindle a fire under the cauldron of rebirth. And then the corpses were thrown into the cauldron, until it was full, and they would rise up the next morning as fighting men as good as before, except they could not speak.

And then, when Efnisien saw the corpses, without any of the men of the Island of the Mighty being put in the same place, he thought to himself, 'Oh God,' he said, 'alas that I should be the cause of this heap of the men of the Island of the Mighty, and shame to me,' he said, 'if I do not seek deliverance from this.' And he crept in among the corpses of the Irish, and two bare-bottomed Irishmen[36] came and threw him into the cauldron as if he were an Irishman. He stretched himself out in the cauldron so that the cauldron burst into four pieces, and so that his own heart burst.

And from that there was such victory as there was for the men of the Island of the Mighty. There was no victory from that except the escape of seven men, and Bendigeidfran was wounded in the foot with a poisoned spear. These are the seven men who escaped – Pryderi, Manawydan, Glifiau eil Taran,[37] Taliesin,[38] and Ynawg, Gruddiau son of Muriel, Heilyn son of Gwyn the Old.

And then Bendigeidfran had his own head cut off. 'And take the head,' he said, 'and bring it as far as the White Hill in London, and bury it with its face toward France. And you will be a long time on the road – in Harddlech you will be feasting for seven years, with the birds of Rhiannon singing to you. And the companionship of the head will be as good to you as it ever was to you at best, when it was on me. And you will be in Gwales in Penfro[39] for fourscore years. And until you open the door facing Aber Henfelen, the side toward Cornwall, you can stay there, and the head with you uncorrupted. But from the time you open that door, you can not stay there. Make for London to bury the head. And set out now for the other side.'

Aber Alaw.
Sea pink in
flower near
the mouth
(*aber*) of
the Alaw.

Bedd Branwen.
The Bronze-Age
burial mound known
as the grave (*bedd*)
of Branwen in Glan
Alaw. The infant Alaw
runs beside the fence
in the background.

And then his head was struck off, and these seven, with Branwen as the eighth, set out with the head for the other side. And at Aber Alaw in Talebolion they came to land. And there they sat and rested.

She looked from there upon Ireland and upon the Island of the Mighty, what could be seen of them. 'Oh, Son of God,' she cried, 'alas for my birth! Two good islands have been destroyed because of me.' And she gave a great sigh, and upon that her heart broke. And a four-sided grave was made for her, and she was buried there in Glan Alaw.[40]

And upon that the seven men travelled toward Harddlech, and the head with them. As they were travelling, behold, a company of men and women met with them.

'Do you have news?' asked Manawydan.

'No,' they replied, 'except that Caswallawn son of Beli has conquered the Island of the Mighty, and he is crowned king in London.'

'What happened,' they asked, 'to Cradawg son of Brân and the seven men who were left with him on this island?'

'Caswallawn fell upon them, and he killed six of the men, and Cradawg himself broke his heart from bewilderment at seeing a sword killing the men, though he did not know who was killing them. Caswallawn had put a magic cloak about himself, and no one could see him slaying

[40] A Bronze Age burial mound, from about 1400 B.C, has been known as *Ynys Bronwen* (Bronwen's Island), *Bedd Bronwen*, or *Bedd Branwen* ('B.'s Grave) at least since the late 18th century; see Bromwich, *Trioedd*, pp. 287, 545-46.

Harddlech.
Looking southwest
toward Harlech
Castle silhouetted in
the afternoon light.

the men, except for the sword. Caswallawn did not wish to kill him – he was his nephew, his cousin's son. And he was one of the Three People who Broke their Hearts from Bewilderment.[41] Pendaran Dyfed, who was a young lad with the seven men, escaped to the wood,' they said.[42]

And then they made for Harddlech, and they began to sit, and they began to be supplied abundantly with food and drink. And as they began to eat and drink, three birds came and began singing to them a kind of song, and whatever they had heard of song, each one was

unpleasant compared to that. And it was far for them to see those birds out over the sea, but they were as clear to them as if they were right with them. And they were at that feast for seven years.

And at the end of the seventh year, they set out for Gwales in Penfro. And there was a fair kingly place for them above the sea, and there was a great hall, and they made their way to the hall. And they could see two open doors. A third door was closed, the one facing Cornwall.

'Behold yonder,' said Manawydan, 'the door we ought not to open.' And that night they were

Gwales.
The island of Grassholm, just visible on the horizon beyond the rocks of Skomer Island, is possibly the location of the mysterious Gwales.

[41] No early version of this triad has survived, but in 1717 Moses Williams included the following in his collection of triads: 'Three People who broke their hearts from bewilderment: Branwen daughter of Llŷr, and Caradog son of Brân, and Ffaraon Dandde;' Bromwich, *Trioedd*, number 95. In the separate story of *Lludd and Llefelys*, there is a reference to Ffaraon Dandde as one of three stewards who broke their hearts from bewilderment.

[42] 'Shame on your beard!' was a serious insult to one's manhood. In medieval Welsh law, a husband is not subject to a fine if he strikes his wife for saying this. (On the other hand, she can divorce him for bad breath.)

there, lacking nothing, and it was pleasant to them. And despite what they had ever seen of grief, and of what they themselves had suffered, no memory of it came to them, neither of that, nor of any sorrow in the world. And there they passed fourscore years, such that they never knew of spending a period of time more joyful or more pleasant than that. No more irksome was it, nor could any one tell that the others were older in that much time, than when they came there. No more irksome was it for them dwelling with the head then, than when Bendigeidfran had been alive with them. And because of those fourscore years, it was called 'the Assembly of the Noble Head'. The Assembly of Branwen and Matholwch was that which had gone to Ireland.

This is what Heilyn son of Gwyn did one day – 'Shame on my beard,' he said, 'if I do not open the door to find out whether it is true what is said about that.'[42]

He opened the door and looked on Cornwall and on Aber Henfelen. And when he looked, as many losses as they had ever lost, and as many kin and companions as they had lost, and as many evils as had come to them were as clear to them as if it were just then they had met with them, and above all because of their lord. And from that moment they were unable to rest, unless they set out with the head toward London.

However long they were on the road, they reached London and they buried the head in the White Hill. And that was one of the Three Fortunate Concealments when it was concealed, and one of the Three Unfortunate Disclosures when it was disclosed, since no oppression would ever come over the sea to this island while the head was in that concealment.[43] And this tale tells of that. That is their adventure, the men who set out from Ireland.

In Ireland not a person was left alive, except five pregnant women in a cave in the wilderness of Ireland. And those five women, at the same time, gave birth to five sons. And they raised those five sons until they were large youths, and they thought about women, and they had a desire to have them. And then each one slept higgledy-piggledy with the mother of his fellow, and ruled the land and peopled it, and divided it among all five. And because of that division, the five provinces of Ireland are still so called. And they searched the land where battles had been, and found gold and silver, until they were wealthy.

and that is how this branch of THE MABINOGI ends

concerning the Blow to Branwen — this was one of the Three Unfortunate Blows in this island, and concerning the Assembly of Brân — when a host from seven score and fourteen lands went to Ireland to avenge the Blow to Branwen, and about the feast in Harddlech for seven years, and about the Singing of Rhiannon's Birds and about the Assembly of the Head for fourscore years.

[43] The triad of the 'Three Concealments and Three Disclosures of the Island of Britain' is found in the *White Book*, but the longer version in the *Red Book of Hergest* is closer to the text of *The Mabinogi*: 'Three Fortunate Concealments of the Island of Britain: The Head of Brân the Blessed, son of Llŷr, which was concealed in the White Hill in London, with its face toward France. And as long as it was in the position in which it was put there, no Saxon Oppression would ever come to this Island; The second Fortunate Concealment: the Dragons in Dinas Emrys, which Lludd son of Beli concealed; And the third: the Bones of Gwerthefyr the Blessed [=Vortimer], in the Chief Ports of this Island. And as long as they remained in that concealment, no Saxon Oppression would ever come to this Island. And they were the Three Unfortunate Disclosures when these were disclosed. And Gwrtheyrn the Thin [=Vortigern] disclosed the bones of Gwrthefyr the Blessed for the love of a woman: that was Ronnwen the pagan woman; And it was he who disclosed the Dragons; And Arthur disclosed the head of Brân the Blessed from the White Hill because it did not seem right to him that this Island should be defended by the strength of anyone, but by his own;' Bromwich, *Trioedd*, number 37R. This triad, like several early Irish and Latin references, may record a memory of talismanic burial among the Celtic peoples.

Harddlech sunset.
The Llŷn Peninsula,
seen from Harlech, is
highlighted by the
setting sun.

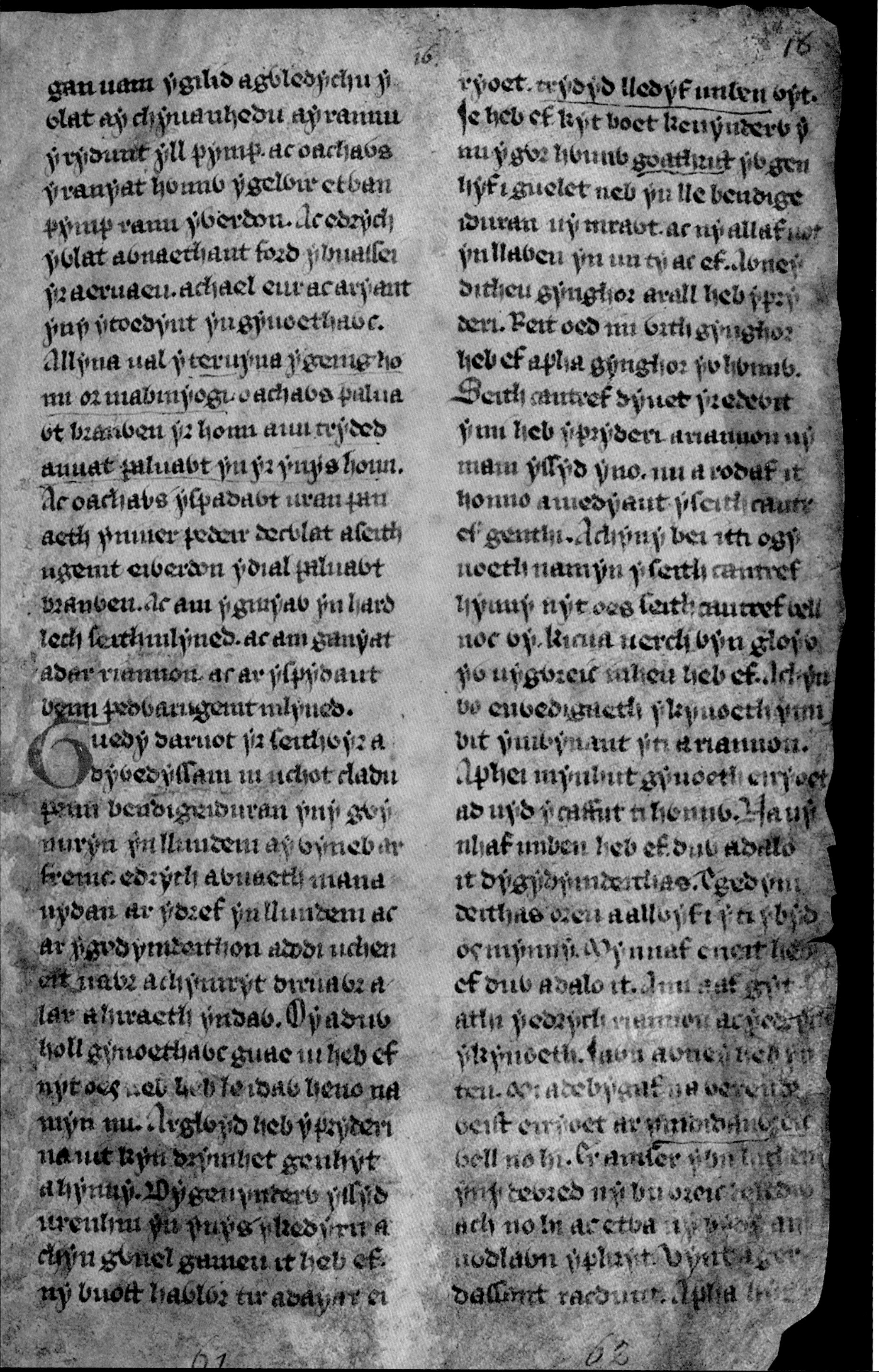

here is the third branch of THE MABINOGI

[44] For the legal overtones of 'land and earth,' see note 9. The triad referred to is 'Three Prostrate Chieftains of the Island of Britain: Llywarch the Old son of Elidir Llydanwyn, and Manawydan son of Llŷr Half-Speech, and Gwgon Gwron son of Peredur son of Eliffer of the Great Retinue. (And this is why those were called 'Prostrate Chieftains': because they would not seek a dominion, which nobody could deny to them;' Rachel Bromwich, *Trioedd*, number 8. I have translated *lledyf*, literally 'slanting, oblique, declining', as 'resigned;' Bromwich translates it as 'prostrate,' in the sense of 'laid low by misfortune' (p. lxxxix). Other possibilities, depending on one's interpretation of this episode and of Manawydan's character, include 'ungrasping,' 'humble,' 'gentle,' 'impassive,' 'obedient,' or 'melancholy.' The main point is that Manawydan does not insist on regaining his rightful inheritance.

AFTER the seven men we spoke of above buried the head of Bendigeidfran in the White Hill in London, with its face toward France, Manawydan looked upon the town in London and upon his companions and gave a great sigh, and he felt immense sorrow and longing within him.

'Oh, Almighty God, alas for me!' he said. 'There is none without a place for him tonight except me.'

'Lord,' said Pryderi, 'do not be as heavy-hearted as that. Your cousin is king in the Island of the Mighty, and though he has done wrong to you,' he said, 'you have never been a claimant for land and earth – you are one of the Three Resigned Chieftains.'[44]

'Yea,' he replied, 'though that man may be my cousin, I am sad to see anyone in place of Bendigeidfran, my brother, and I can not be happy in the same house as he.'

'Will you take other counsel?' asked Pryderi.

'I was in need of counsel,' he said, 'and what counsel is that?'

'The seven cantrefs of Dyfed have been left to me,' said Pryderi, 'and my mother,

Rhiannon, is there. I will give her, and the authority over the seven cantrefs, to you. And though you would have no realm except those seven cantrefs, there are no better cantrefs than they. Cigfa daughter of Gwyn Gloyw is my wife,' he said. 'And though the title to the realm is mine, let the enjoyment of it be yours and Rhiannon's. And if you ever wished for a realm, perhaps you will take that.'

'I don't wish for it,' he replied. 'May God repay you your friendship.'

'The best friendship I can give will be yours, if you wish it.'

'I do, friend,' he said. 'May God repay you. And I will go with you to look upon Rhiannon and to view the realm.'

'You do right,' he answered. 'I suspect you have never listened to a woman better at conversation than she. Since the time she was in her prime, there was no woman more beautiful than she, and still her appearance is not displeasing.'

They travelled on, and however long they were on the road, they came to Dyfed. There was a feast prepared for them, awaiting their arrival in Arberth, which Rhiannon and Cigfa had made ready.

And then Manawydan and Rhiannon began to sit together and to converse. And from the conversation, his mind and thought grew tender toward her, and he delighted in his thought that he had never seen a woman better endowed in her fairness and her beauty than she.

'Pryderi,' he said, 'I will abide by what you stated.'

'What statement was that?' asked Rhiannon.

'Lady,' said Pryderi, 'I have given you as a wife to Manawydan son of Llŷr.'

'And I will abide by that gladly,' said Rhiannon.

'I, too, am glad,' said Manawydan. 'And may God repay the man who is granting to me his friendship as steadfast as that.' Before that feast came to an end, he slept with her.

'You partake of whatever is left of the feast,'

Dyfed. Looking across Dyfed from Carningli in the Preseli Hills.

Gorsedd Arberth. The natural mound known as Crug Mawr or Banc y Warren, a suggested site of Gorsedd Arberth, as seen from the remains of Crug Llwyn Llwyd hillfort.

[45] *Lloegr* is the Welsh name for England, originally perhaps the Midland region which Anglo-Saxons called Mercia. It appears in French and Middle English Arthurian legend as *Logres*. To the characters in the tale, *Lloegr* is a Celtic realm; by the storyteller's time it had become England.

[46] For *gorsedd* '(burial) mound' and for suggested sites of Gorsedd Arberth, see note 10.

said Pryderi, 'and I will go to tender my homage to Caswallawn son of Beli in Lloegr.'[45]

'Lord,' said Rhiannon, 'Caswallawn is in Kent, and you may partake of this feast and wait for him until he is nearer.'

'We will wait for him,' he replied, and they partook of that feast.

And they began a circuit of Dyfed, and hunted it, and took their pleasure. And while going about the land, they had never seen a land more habitable than it, nor better hunting land, nor more plentiful in its honey or its fish than it. And upon that a friendship grew among those four so that not one of them wished to be without the other either day or night. And amongst that, he went to Caswallawn in Oxford

to tender his homage to him. And he was met there with great joy, and thanks to him for tendering his homage to him, and after he returned, Pryderi and Manawydan resumed their feasts and their comfort.

And they began a feast in Arberth, since it was a chief court and all honour originated from there. And after the first serving that night, while the servants were eating, they went out and those four made for Gorsedd Arberth,[46] and a retinue together with them.

And as they were sitting thus, behold, a tumult, and with the extent of the tumult, behold, a mist settled so that not one of them could see the other. And after the mist, behold, it grew light everywhere, and when they looked to where they used to see the flocks and herds and inhabited places before that, no one could see anything at all – neither house nor animal nor smoke nor fire nor person nor inhabited place, but the houses of the court empty, desolate, uninhabited, without a person, without an animal in them, their own companions lost, without knowing anything about them, except for those four.

'Oh, Lord God,' cried Manawydan. 'Where is the retinue of the court and our company except for this? Let us go to see.'

They came to the hall – there was no one. Making for the chamber and the sleeping quarters, they saw no one. In the mead cellar and in the kitchen there was nothing but desolation.

Those four began to feast, and they hunted and took their pleasure. And each of them began to go about the land and the realm to see if they could perceive either a house or an inhabited place. But they could see nothing but wild animals. And after they consumed their feast and their provisions, they began to support themselves on meat from the hunt and fish and beehives. And thus they spent a year pleasantly, and a second. But in the end they grew dissatisfied.

'God knows,' said Manawydan, 'we will not be like this. Let us make for Lloegr and seek a craft we might take up to support ourselves.'

They made for Lloegr and came as far as Hereford, and they took up saddle making. And Manawydan himself began to fashion pommels and to colour them in the way he had seen done by Llassar Llaes Gygnwyd with blue enamel. And he made blue enamel for it as the other man had done. And because of that it is still called *calch llassar* because it was made by Llassar Llaes Gygnwyd.[47]

And because of that work, while it could be had from Manawydan, neither pommel nor saddle was bought from a saddler across the face of Hereford, so that each one of the saddlers knew he was losing his earnings, and nothing was bought from them except after it could not be had from Manawydan. And with that, they gathered together and agreed on killing him and his companion. And with that they received warning, and took counsel about leaving the town.

'Between me and God,' said Pryderi, 'I do not counsel leaving town – rather kill those churls yonder.'

'No,' replied Manawydan, 'if we were to fight with them, we would have ill fame and would be imprisoned. It is better for us,' he said, 'to make for another town in which to support ourselves.' And then the four of them made for another city.

'What craft,' asked Pryderi, 'shall we take upon us?'

'We will make shields,' replied Manawydan.

'Do we know anything about that?' asked Pryderi.

'We will try it,' he answered.

They began the shield work, fashioning them according to the work of good shields they had seen, and they put the colour on them that they had put on the saddles. And that work succeeded for them so that no shield was bought in the entire town until after it could not be had from them. Their work was swift and they made an immeasurable amount.

[47] *calch llassar* 'blue enamel': the storyteller gives his own etymological speculation here, as elsewhere. In medieval Welsh laws enumerating the value of various items, we find 'a shield, eightpence; if it has blue enamel or gold enamel (*kalch llassar neu eurgalch*), twenty-four pence.' Dafydd Jenkins, *The Law of Hywel Dda*, p. 194. One law text also mentions coloured saddles, but does not specify this particular term. *Calch* also means 'lime, chalk,' which might have been the medium for mixing the colouring. *Llassar* may derive ultimately from Persian *lázhward* 'lapis lazuli,' or from Old Irish *lasar* 'flame,' in the sense of 'bright, shining.' For variants of Llassar's name, see note 28.

Hereford.
The Black Hill in Herefordshire looks across the Olchon Valley to the Welsh border, which runs along the escarpment of the Black Mountains.

And they were thus until their fellow townsmen became angry toward them, and they agreed to try to kill them. Warning came to them and they heard that the men were of a mind to put them to death.

'Pryderi,' said Manawydan, 'these men wish to destroy us.'

'We will not take that from those churls. Let us fall upon them and kill them.'

'No,' he replied, 'Caswallawn would hear of that, and his men, and we would be ruined. We shall make for another town.'

They came to another town.

'What craft shall we turn to?' asked Manawydan.

'Whichever you wish of those we know,' said Pryderi.

'No,' he replied, 'we will take up

shoemaking. Shoemakers will not have the heart either to fight with us or to hinder us.'

'I know nothing about that,' said Pryderi.

'I know it,' said Manawydan, 'and I will teach you to stitch. And we will not concern ourselves with preparing leather, but will buy it ready and make our work from it.'

And then he began to buy the finest Cordovan leather he found in the town. And he would not buy leather other than that except for leather for soles. And he began to befriend the best goldsmith in the town and he had buckles made for the boots and the buckles gilded, and he himself observed that carefully until he learned it. And because of that he was called one of the Three Golden Shoemakers.[48] While it could be had from him, no boots nor leggings were bought at all from a shoemaker in the whole town. This is what the shoemakers did – they knew that their earnings were flagging for them, since as Manawydan fashioned the work, Pryderi would sew it. The shoemakers came and took counsel. This is what they decided in their council – they agreed on killing them.

'Pryderi,' said Manawydan, 'the men wish to kill us.'

'Why do we take that from the thieving churls,' said Pryderi, 'rather than killing them all.'

'No,' replied Manawydan, 'we shall not fight with them, and we shall not remain in Lloegr any longer. We shall make for Dyfed and go to look upon it.'

However long they were on the road, they came to Dyfed, and they made for Arberth. And they struck a fire, and began to support

themselves with hunting, and they spent a month in that manner. And they gathered their hounds to them and hunted, and they were there in that manner for a year.

And one morning Pryderi and Manawydan arose to hunt. And they prepared their hounds and went outside the court. This is what some of their hounds did – they ran ahead of them and went into a small thicket that was near at hand.[49] And just as they go into the thicket, they retreat quickly, with a great, terrible hair-raising fear upon them, and they return to the men.

'Let us draw near,' said Pryderi, 'to the thicket to see what is in it.'

They drew near to the thicket. As they drew near, behold, a shining white wild boar arising from the thicket. This is what the hounds did, taking courage from the men – they rushed it. This is what it did – it left the thicket and retreated a little way from the men. And until the men would come close to it, it would hold the hounds at bay, without retreating before them. And when the men would come near, it would retreat again and break away.

And they followed after the boar until they could see a great high fort, with new work upon it, where they had never seen either stone or work. And the boar made for the fort swiftly, with the hounds after it. And after the boar and the hounds went into the fort, they marvelled at seeing a fort in a place they had never seen construction before that. And from the top of the mound they looked and listened for the hounds. However long they were thus, they

[48] 'Three Golden Shoemakers of the Island of Britain: Caswallawn son of Beli, when he went to Rome to seek Fflur; and Manawydan son of Llŷr, when the Enchantment was on Dyfed; and Lleu Skilful-Hand, when he and Gwydion were seeking a name and arms from his mother Aranrhod;' Rachel Bromwich, *Trioedd*, number 67. The story of Lleu is told in the Fourth Branch. The story of Caswallawn and Fflur has not survived, though there are several references to it by poets from the 12th to the 14th century.

[49] thicket: The name *Arberth* means 'by or near the thicket,' from *perth* 'thicket, copse;' perhaps originally a copse of oak, for *perth* derives from the Indo-European root meaning 'oak.'

did not hear one of the hounds nor anything about them.

'Lord,' said Pryderi, 'I will go into the fort to seek news of the hounds.'

'God knows,' he replied, 'your counsel is not good – to go into the fort. We never saw this fort here, and if you will take my counsel, you will not go into it.[50] And the one who placed an enchantment on the land caused the fort to be here.'

'God knows,' said Pryderi, 'I will not abandon my hounds.'

Whatever counsel he got from Manawydan, he made for the fort. When he came to the fort, neither man nor animal, nor the boar nor the hounds, nor house nor habitation could he see in the fort. He could see, about the centre of the grounds of the fort, a fountain with marble work around it. And on the edge of the fountain, a basin above a slab of marble, with chains rising into the air, and he could not see the end of them.[51] He marvelled at the fairness of the gold and the excellence of the work of the basin. And he came where the basin was and grasped it. And as soon as he grasps the basin, his hands stick to the basin and his feet to the slab he was standing on, and his speech[52] is taken from him so that he could not say a single word. And thus he stood.

Manawydan waited for him until near the end of the day. And late in the afternoon, after he was certain he would not have news from Pryderi, nor from the hounds, he came toward the court. When he came in, this is what Rhiannon did – she looked at him.

'Where,' she said, 'is your friend, and your hounds?'

'Here,' he answered, 'is my tale,' and he related it all.

'God knows,' said Rhiannon, 'a bad friend have you been, and a good friend have you lost.'

And with that word, she went out, and she set out in the direction that he had said the man and the fort were. She saw the gate of the fort open; there was no concealment on it. And she came in, and as she came, she beheld Pryderi grasping the basin and came to him.

'Alas, my lord,' she cried, 'what are you doing here?' And she grasped the basin with him. And as soon as she grasps it, her hands stick to the basin, and her feet to the slab, so that she could not say a single word.

And upon that, as soon as it was night, behold a great tumult about them, and a shower of mist, and with that the fort disappeared, and away with them, too.

When Cigfa daughter of Gwyn Gloyw, Pryderi's wife, saw there was no one in the court except for her and Manawydan, she lamented that it was no better for her to live than to die. This is what Manawydan did – he observed that.

'God knows,' he said, 'you are wrong about me, if you lament for fear of me. I will give God as surety to you, you have not seen a more true friend than you will have in me, for as long as God wills you to be thus. Between me and God, though I were in the spring of my youth, I would keep trust with Pryderi, and for your sake I would keep it. And let there be not a single fear upon you,' he said. 'Between me and God,' he said, 'you shall have the friendship you wish from me, to the best of my ability,

50 The clause 'We never saw this fort here' has been taken from the earliest manuscript fragment of the tale, Peniarth 6. The White Book scribe's eye seems to have skipped from *caer* 'fort' at the end of the preceding sentence to the same word at the end of this clause, giving the less satisfactory reading 'to go into this fort here, and if….'

51 The Peniarth 6 manuscript is more detailed: 'a gold basin bound by four chains, and that above a slab of marble, and the chains rising into the air, and no end of them in the world could he see.'

52 The White Book and the Red Book both read *llywenydd* 'joy,' which is defensible, given *gorawenu* 'rejoiced' just above. Peniarth 6, however, reads *lleferydd* 'speech,' rather than *lywenydd* 'joy,' and *gorfynnu* 'marvelled' instead of *gorawenu* 'rejoiced.' Both of these readings suit the context somewhat better than the White and Red Book readings. Note how the narrator slips into the present tense to convey the suddenness with which Pryderi is trapped.

while God may see fit for us to be in this wretchedness and care.'

'May God repay you, and that is what I supposed.' And then the young woman gained in joy and confidence because of that.

'Yea, friend,' said Manawydan, 'here is not a suitable place for us to live. We lost our hounds and we cannot support ourselves. Let us make for Lloegr – it is easiest to support ourselves there.'

'Gladly, lord,' she replied, 'and we will do that.' Together they travelled toward Lloegr. 'Lord,' she said, 'What craft will you take upon you? Take a clean one.'

Lloegr. The Hereford Plain in Lloegr (England) as seen from the Black Hill.

'I will take up nothing,' he answered, 'except shoemaking, as we did before.'

'Lord,' she said, 'that is not acceptable in its cleanliness for a man of such skill, of such rank as you.'

'By that will I go,' he said.

He began his craft, and he prepared his work from the finest Cordovan leather he could get in the town. And as they had begun in the other place, he began to buckle the shoes with golden buckles, so that the work of all the shoemakers of the town was vain and inferior compared to his own. And while it could be had from him, neither shoe nor hose was bought from others at all.

And he spent a year there thus, so that the shoemakers felt malice and envy toward him, and until warnings came to him, saying that the shoemakers had agreed to kill him.

'Lord,' said Cigfa, 'why is this tolerated from the churls?'

'It is not so!' he said. 'We could go, nevertheless, to Dyfed.'

They made for Dyfed. This is what Manawydan did when he set out for Dyfed – he took a load of wheat with him, and made for Arberth and settled there. And there was nothing more pleasant to him than to see Arberth and the territory he used to hunt, he and Pryderi and Rhiannon together with them. He began to become accustomed there to hunting fish and animals in their lair. And after that, he began to till the soil, and after that to sow a croft, and a second, and a third.[53] And behold, the wheat coming up the best in the world, and his three crofts flourishing with the same growth, so that man had not seen finer wheat than it.

He spent the seasons of the year. Behold, the autumn came, and he came to look at one of his crofts. Behold, that one was ripe.

'I intend to reap this tomorrow,' he said. He came back that night to Arberth.

In the pale dawn the next day he came intending to reap the croft. When he came, there was nothing but the stalks, bare – each one had been broken off where the ear came out of the stalk, and the grain was all taken away, and the stalks were left there bare. He marvelled at that greatly and came to look at another croft. Behold, that one was ripe.

'God knows,' he said, 'I intend to reap this tomorrow.'

And the next day he came, thinking to reap that. And when he came, there was nothing but the bare stalks.

'Oh, Lord God,' he cried, 'who is bringing about my ruin? And I know who – the one who began my ruin is bringing it about, and he destroyed the land along with me.'

He came to look at the third croft. When he came, no man had seen finer wheat, and that was ripe.

'Shame on me,' he said, 'if I do not watch tonight. Whatever took the other corn will come to take this, and I shall know what it is.' And he took his arms and began watching the croft. And he told all that to Cigfa.

'Yea,' she said, 'what is in your mind?'

'I will watch the croft tonight,' he answered. He went to watch the croft.

And as he was thus at about midnight, behold

[53] A croft is an enclosed field. The Welsh text uses the forms *groft* and *grofd;* this is the earliest known use in Welsh of this word, borrowed from Old English.

the greatest tumult in the world. This is what he did – he looked. Lo, there was greatest host of mice in the world, and neither number nor measure of that could be reckoned. And before he knew it the mice were rushing through the croft, and each one climbing along a stalk and bending down with it and breaking off the ear and rushing away with the grain and leaving the stalks there. And for all he knew there was not a single stalk there without a mouse for each one, and they went on their way, and the grain with them.

And then between anger and rage, he struck amongst the mice. But no more than among gnats or birds in the air could he keep an eye on any one of them, except for a very fat one which he could see, that he supposed was incapable of any fleetfootedness. He went after that one, and he caught it, and he put it in his glove and with a string tied the opening of the glove and kept it with him and made for the court.

He came to the chamber where Cigfa was and lit the fire, and with the string he put the glove on a peg.

'What is there, lord?' asked Cigfa.

'A thief,' he said, 'which I caught stealing from me.'

'What sort of thief, lord, could you put in your glove?' she asked.

'Here it all is,' he answered, and he told how his crofts had been damaged and spoiled, and how the mice came to the last croft in his very sight. 'And one of them was very fat, and I caught it, and it is in the glove, and I will hang it myself tomorrow. And by my confession to God, if I had caught them all, I would hang them.'

'Lord,' she said, 'that was not surprising. But nevertheless it is unpleasant to see a man of such rank, of such nobility as you hanging that sort of creature. And if you would do right, you would not concern yourself with the creature, but let it go.'

'Shame on me,' he replied, 'if I had caught them all, if I wouldn't hang them – and what I have caught, I will hang it.'

'Yea, lord,' she said, 'there is no cause for me to be of help to that creature, except to keep discourtesy from you. But do your own will, lord.'

'If I knew any reason in the world that you ought to be of help to it, I would abide by your counsel about it. But since I know none, lady, my thought is to destroy it.'

'Do as you wish gladly,' she replied.

And then he made for Gorsedd Arberth, and the mouse with him. And he pushed down two forks on the highest part of the mound. And as he was thus, lo, he could see a cleric coming towards him with poor old threadbare clothes upon him. And it had been seven years before that since he had seen either man or beast, except for the four people that had been together – until the two were lost.

'Lord,' said the cleric, 'good day to you.'

'May God prosper you, and welcome to you,' he replied. 'Where do you come from, cleric?' he said.

'I come from singing in Lloegr. And why do you ask, lord?' he said.

'I have not seen,' he answered, 'for seven years a single person here except four exiled people, and now you.'

'Yea, lord, I am going,' he said, 'through this land now toward my own land. And what sort of work are you doing, lord?'

'Hanging a thief I caught stealing from me,' he said.

'What kind of thief, lord?' he asked. 'I see a creature in your hand, like a mouse, and it ill suits a man of such rank as you to touch a creature of that sort. Let it go.'

'I will not, between me and God,' said he. 'I caught it stealing, and the law of a thief will I carry out with it: to hang it.'[54]

'Lord,' said he, 'rather than see a man of such rank as you at that work, a pound which I received from begging alms I will give to you, and you let that creature go.'

'I will not, between me and God; I will not sell it.'

'Do as you wish, lord,' he said. 'If it were not unsightly to see a man of such rank as you handling that sort of creature, it would not matter to me.' And away went the cleric.

As he was placing the crossbar in the forks, behold, a priest coming towards him on a well-equipped horse.

'Lord, good day to you,' he said.

'May God prosper you,' said Manawydan, 'and your blessing.'

'God's blessing to you. And what sort of work, lord, are you doing?'

'Hanging a thief I caught stealing from me,' he said.

'What sort of thief, lord?' he asked.

'A creature,' said he, 'in the form of a mouse, and it was stealing from me, and a thief's death will I carry out upon it.'

'Lord, rather than see you touching that creature, I will buy it. Let it go.'

'To God I give my confession, I will neither sell it nor let it go.'

'It is true, lord, there is no price upon it at all. Rather than see you defiling yourself with that creature, I will give you three pounds, and you let it go.'

'I do not wish, between me and God,' said he, 'any price except that which it deserves: to hang it.'

'Gladly, lord, do as you please.' Away went the priest.

This is what he did – he tied the string around the neck of the mouse. And as he was raising it, lo, he could see a bishop's retinue, with his packs and his company, and the bishop himself making his way towards him. This is what he did – he paused in his work.

'Lord Bishop,' he said, 'your blessing.'

'May God give his blessing to you,' he said. 'What sort of work are you doing?'

'Hanging a thief I caught stealing from me,' he said.

'Is it not a mouse,' said he, 'that I see in your hand?'

'Yea,' said he, 'and she was a thief to me.'

'Yea,' said he, 'since I have come at the destruction of that creature, I will buy it from you. I will give you seven pounds for it, rather than see a man of such rank as you destroying a creature as worthless as that. Let it go, and you shall have the goods.'

'I will not, between me and God,' said he.

'Since you will not let it go for that, I will give you twenty-four pounds of ready silver, and you let it go.'

[54] According to medieval Welsh law, theft (taking something by stealth) was a capital crime. Though there were many circumstances in which a lesser punishment was to be exacted, Manawydan caught the 'thief' in the very act, and since there is nothing to be said in its defence, he seems to be carrying out the legal punishment.

'I will not, I give my confession to God, for as much again,' he said.

'Since you will not let it go for that,' he said, 'I will give what you see of horses in this field and seven packs which are here and the seven horses they are on.'

'I will not, between me and God,' said he.

'Since you do not desire that, you set the price.'

'I will,' said he: 'the freeing of Rhiannon and Pryderi.'

'You shall have that.'

'I will not, between me and God.'

'What do you want?'

'Lifting the enchantment and spell from upon the seven cantrefs of Dyfed.'

'You shall have that also, and you let the mouse go.'

'I will not, between me and God,' he said. 'I wish to know who the mouse is.'

'She is my wife, and if that were not so, I would not redeem her.'

'How did she come to me?'

'To pillage,' said he. 'I am Llwyd son of Cil Coed, and I placed the enchantment upon the seven cantrefs of Dyfed, and to revenge Gwawl son of Clud, out of friendship with him, I placed the enchantment. And upon Pryderi I have avenged playing badger-in-a-bag with Gwawl son of Clud when Pwyll Head of Annwfn did that, and he did that from lack of counsel in the court of Hefeydd the Old. And after hearing that you were settled in the land, my warband came to me and asked to be transformed into mice to destroy your corn. And the first night my warband came themselves, and the second night

they came also and they destroyed the two crofts. And the third night my wife and the women of the court came to me to ask me to transform them, and I did. But she was pregnant, and if she had not been pregnant, you would not have caught up with her. But since she was, and she was caught, I will give Pryderi and Rhiannon to you, and I will lift the enchantment and spell from upon Dyfed. I have told you who she is, and now you release her.'

'I will not, between me and God,' he said.

'What is it you want?' he asked.

'Here,' said he, 'is what I want: that there be no enchantment ever on the seven cantrefs of Dyfed, and none placed upon it.'

'You shall have that,' he said, 'and now let her go.'

'I will not, between me and God,' he said.

'What is it you want?' he asked.

'Here,' said he, 'is what I want: that no revenge for this be taken upon Pryderi and Rhiannon, nor upon me, ever.'

'All of that you shall have. And God knows, you have struck well,' he said. 'If you had not struck upon that,' he said, 'all of the trouble would have fallen on your head.'

'Yea,' said he, 'I took care specifically against that.'

'And now set my wife free.'

'I will not, between me and God, until I see Pryderi and Rhiannon free together with me.'

'You can see them coming now,' he said.

And upon that, behold, Pryderi and Rhiannon. He arose to meet them and welcome them, and they sat together.

'Ah, good sir, now free my wife. Now you have gotten all that you specified.'

'I will let her go gladly,' he said.

And then she was released, and the other struck her with a magic wand and she was restored in the shape of the most beautiful young woman anyone had seen.

'Look around you at the land,' he said, 'and you will see all the dwellings and inhabited places as they were at best.'

And then he rose up and looked, and when he looked he could see all the land inhabited and fitted out with its animals and its dwellings.

'What sort of service have Pryderi and Rhiannon been in?' he asked.

'Pryderi would have the hammers of the gate of my court about his neck, and Rhiannon would have the collars of asses, after they had been gathering hay, about her neck. And such was their imprisonment.'

And because of that imprisonment, that tale is called *Mabinogi of Collar and Yoke*.[55]

and thus ends this branch of THE MABINOGI

---

[55] The Welsh *yrdd*, plural of *ordd* 'hammer', is translated as 'hammers,' though we do not know specifically what this refers to – perhaps knockers, bars, or bolts. The storyteller refers to gathering hay because of his understanding of *mynwair* 'collar' as a compound of *mwn* 'neck' plus *gwair* 'hay.' The second element is actually from *gwair* 'bend, curve.' I have translated the obscure word *mynordd* as 'yoke;' the storyteller seems to have understood it more literally as a compound of *mwn* 'neck' and *ordd* 'hammer.' The punishment of Pryderi and Rhiannon seems to have consisted, in part at least, of treating them as beasts of burden. Many scholars see this as further evidence of a connection between Rhiannon and the Celtic horse goddess, Epona.

Dyfed sunset.
Moonrise at sunset on
Carningli Common
in Dyfed.

750 · 751

[56] The location of 'Caer Dathyl in Arfon' is uncertain. Two possible *caerau* (plural of *caer* 'fort') are the Iron-Age hillforts of Craig y Dinas and Caer Engan, about a mile and a half and three miles inland respectively from the west coast of Arfon, both quite near other places named in this branch. Caernarfon is another possibility; though its full name is Caer Saint yn Arfon (see note 26), it has been suggested that Caer Dathyl yn Arfon may have been an alternative early name. However, the occurrence of 'Caer Saint yn Arfon' in the Second Branch argues against this identification.

[57] The *White Book* reads *giluathwy uab don o a euyd uab don o*. The *don o* may represent *Dono*, possibly an earlier version of the name *Dôn*, parallel to that of the Irish goddess *Danu* (see the Afterword, p. 119); elsewhere it appears as *Don*. The *White Book* reading *a euyd* and the *Red Book*'s *ac eueydd* most likely reflect a scribal error for *a gwydyon* 'and Gwydion', though an Efydd, Eufydd, Ewydd (or various other spellings) is known elsewhere as a son of Dôn.

MATH son of Mathonwy was lord of Gwynedd, and Pryderi son of Pwyll was lord of twenty-one cantrefs in the South. This is what they were – seven cantrefs of Dyfed, and seven of Morgannwg, and four of Ceredigion, and three of Ystrad Tywi. And at that time Math son of Mathonwy could not live except while his feet were in the fold of a maiden's lap, unless the tumult of war prevented him. This was the maiden with him – Goewin daughter of Pebin of Dôl Bebin in Arfon. And she was the fairest maiden of her time of all those known then.

And he had his permanent residence in Caer Dathyl[56] in Arfon. And he could not go on the circuit of his land, but Gilfaethwy son of Dôn and Gwydion son of Dôn[57], his nephews, and the household troops with them, went the circuit of the land for him.

this is the fourth branch of
THE MABINOGI

Caer Dathyl. The hillfort of Craig-y-Dinas is one of several possible locations of Caer Dathyl. This view looks across the entrance between the ramparts toward the Nantlle valley.

And the maiden was with Math continually. And Gilfaethwy son of Dôn set his mind on the maiden, and he loved her so that he did not know what to do about her. And behold, his colour and his appearance and his condition declined for love of her, so that it was not easy to recognize him.

This is what Gwydion, his brother, did – he looked at him keenly one day.

'Ah, lad,' he said, 'what has happened to you?'

'Why?' he asked. 'What do you see about me?'

'I see you,' he said, 'losing your looks and your colour. And what has happened to you?'

'Lord brother,' he replied, 'that which has happened to me, it will not benefit me to admit to anyone.'

'What is that, friend?' he asked.

'You know,' said he, 'the remarkable characteristic of Math son of Mathonwy – any whisper whatever, however small, there may be between two men, if the wind meets with it, he will know it.'

'Yea,' said Gwydion, 'say no more. I know your thought – you love Goewin.'

This is what the other did then, when he saw that his brother knew his thought – he heaved the heaviest sigh in the world.

'Silence your sighing, friend,' he said. 'Not by that will it be overcome. I will bring about,' he said, 'since it cannot be done without that, the mustering of Gwynedd and Powys and Deheubarth in order to seek the maiden. You be glad, and I will bring it about for you.'

And upon that they went to Math son of Mathonwy.

'Lord,' said Gwydion, 'I heard that there have come to the South creatures of a kind that never came to this island before.'

'What is their name?' he asked.

'*Hobau*, lord.'[58]

'What kind of animals are those?'

'Small animals. Their meat is better than beef. They are small, and they are changing names. They are now called pigs.'[59]

'Who do they belong to?'

'Pryderi son of Pwyll. They were sent to him from Annwn by Arawn King of Annwn.'[60]

(And there is still kept of that name: *hanner hwch, hanner hob*.)[61]

'Yea,' said he, 'in what manner can they be got from him?'

'I will go as one of twelve, in the guise of bards, lord, to ask for the pigs.'

'He could refuse you,' said he.

'My plan is not bad, lord,' he said. 'I will not come without the pigs.'

'Gladly,' said he, 'go forth.'

He went, and Gilfaethwy, and ten men with them, as far as Ceredigion, to the place which is now called Rhuddlan Teifi. Pryderi had a court there, and in the guise of bards they came in. They were welcomed. Gwydion was placed at Pryderi's right hand that night.

'Yea,' said Pryderi, 'we will be pleased to have a tale from some of the young men yonder.'

'It is our custom, lord,' said Gwydion, 'that the first night one comes to a great man, the chief poet shall speak. I will tell a tale gladly.' Gwydion himself was the best tale teller in the world, and that night he entertained the court

[58] *Hob*, plural *hobau*, pronounced |ˈhôb-ɪ|, 'swine, hog, pig,' seems to have been an archaic or uncommon term even when *The Mabinogi* was composed.

[59] *Moch*, the word used here, is the usual Welsh term for 'pigs, swine.'

[60] Among the Triads we find 'Three Powerful Swineherds of the Island of Britain: Pryderi son of Pwyll, Lord of Annwfn, tending the swine of Penndaran Dyfed his foster-father. These swine were the seven animals which Pwyll Lord of Annwfn brought, and gave them to Penndaran Dyfed his foster-father. And the place where he used to keep them was in Glyn Cuch in Emlyn. And this is why he was called a Powerful Swineherd: because no one was able either to deceive him or to force him;' Bromwich, *Trioedd*, number 26W.

[61] The narrator explains *hobau* in an aside citing the idiomatic or proverbial phrase *hanner hwch, hanner hob,* pronounced |hän-er **hookh**, hän-er **hôb**|. The compound *hanner hob,* literally 'half a hog', survived in modern Welsh as *hanerob, nerob,* and *norob,* 'a flitch or side of bacon'. *Hanner hwch,* not known elsewhere as a compound, uses a synonym, *hwch,* originally 'swine', but which came to mean more specifically 'sow'. Thus, *hanner hwch, hanner hob,* 'half swine, half hog', or 'a side of bacon, a side of ham', might mean something like 'six of one, half dozen of the other'. Another, if perhaps less likely, interpretation plays on the gender distinction, or confusion, between *hwch* and *hob* – 'half sow, half hog'. The meaning or connotation of such a rendering would be obscure, but it is worth noting if only because gender becomes an important theme in this branch of *The Mabinogi.* From this point on, the text uses *moch,* translated as 'pigs,' and restricts *hwch* to mean 'sow.'

Rhuddlan Teifi. The possible location of Pryderi's court in the Teifi valley is marked by the prominent mound known as Crug y Chwil, which can be seen to the right.

with pleasant conversation and tales, so that it was praiseworthy to all of the court, and Pryderi was pleased to converse with him.

At the end of that, 'Lord,' he said, 'is it better for anyone to tell my errand to you than I myself?'

'It is not,' said he. 'Yours is a quite good tongue.'

'Here then is my errand, lord – to beg you for the animals that were sent to you from Annwn.'

'Yea,' said he, 'that would be the easiest thing in the world if there were not a compact between me and my country regarding them. This is what it is – they should not go from me until they breed twice as many in the land.'

'Lord,' said he, 'I am able to free you from those words. This is how I can do it – do not give me the pigs tonight, but do not refuse them to me. Tomorrow I will show an exchange for them.'

And that night they went, he and his companions, to their lodgings for a council.

'Ah, men,' he said, 'we won't get the pigs by asking for them.'

'Yea,' said they, 'by what plan can they be got?'

'I will manage to get them,' said Gwydion. And then he went into his arts and he began to show his magic. And he conjured up twelve steeds and twelve hunting hounds, each of

Mochdref. The Nant y Moch ('Stream of the Pigs') reservoir preserves the swine-related name that best suits the location of an otherwise unknown Mochdref in the uplands of Ceredigion.

them black with a white breast, with twelve collars and twelve leashes on them, and anyone who saw them would not know they were not gold. And twelve saddles on the horses, and for each place that iron ought to be on them, it was all of gold, and the bridles of the same work as that.

With the horses and with the hounds he came to Pryderi.

'Good day to you, lord,' he said.

'May God prosper you,' he replied, 'and welcome to you.'

'Lord,' he said, 'here is your release from the word you spoke last night about the pigs, that you would not give them and would not sell them. You can make an exchange for what will be better. I will give you these twelve horses, as they are equipped, with their saddles and their reins, and the twelve hunting hounds with their collars and their leashes, as you see them, and the twelve golden shields you see yonder.' (He had conjured those out of toadstools.)

'Yea,' said he, 'we will take counsel.' This is what they arrived at in the council – to give the pigs to Gwydion and to take the horses and the dogs and the shields from him.

[62] Literally, 'Pigtown'; compare the English Swindon, 'swine-town'. There is no known Mochdref in upper Ceredigion, but the name Nant-y-Moch ('stream or vale of the pigs') survives as the name of a modern reservoir in a location that suits the narrative.

Elenid. Elenid or Elenydd, the uplands of Ceredigion.

Ceri. An ancient trackway leads across the hills above the present town of Ceri.

[63] Elenid or Elenydd is the mountainous region around Pumlumon mountain. In his *Journey through Wales*, Giraldus Cambrensis describes taking the same route over Elenid and across Arwystli to Ceri in 1188.

[64] The village of Mochdre, between Newtown and Caersws, is very near to the border between the cantref of Arwystli and the commot of Ceri.

And then they took their leave, and they began to journey with the pigs.

'Ah, champions,' said Gwydion, 'it is necessary for us to journey swiftly. The magic will not last except from one day to another.' And that night they journeyed as far as the uplands of Ceredigion, the place which is still called, because of that, Mochdref.[62] And the next day they took their way; over Elenid they came.[63] And that night they were between Ceri and Arwystli, in the town which is also called, because of that, Mochdref.[64] And from there

Mochdref
(Mochdre).
The village of
Mochdre lies
near the border
between Arwystli
and the commot
of Ceri.

Arwystli.
Overlooking Llyn
Bugeilyn and the
hills of Arwystli.

they went on, and that night they went as far as a commot in Powys which is called, also for the same reason, Mochnant,[65] and they were there that night. And from there they journeyed as far as the cantref of Rhos, and they were there that night in the town which is still called Mochdref.[66]

'Ah, men,' said Gwydion, 'we will make for the fastness of Gwynedd with these animals. There is a host gathering behind us.' This is where they made for – the highest town of Arllechwedd, and there they made a sty for the pigs. And because of that the town was called Creuwrion.[67] And then after they made the sty for the pigs, they made their way to Math son of Mathonwy, as far as Caer Dathyl. And when they came there, the land was being mustered.

'What news is here?' asked Gwydion.

'Pryderi is mustering twenty-one cantrefs after you,' they said. 'It was a marvel how slowly you travelled.'

'Where are the animals you went after?' asked Math.

'They are in the other cantref below, where sty has been made for them,' said Gwydion. Upon that, behold they could hear the trumpets and the mustering in the land. At that, they took arms and went forth until they reached Pennardd in Arfon.

And that night Gwydion son of Dôn returned with Gilfaethwy his brother to Caer Dathyl. And in the bed of Math son of Mathonwy, Gilfaethwy and Goewin daughter of Pebin were placed to sleep together, and the maidens were forced out rudely, and she was slept with against her will that night.

When they saw day on the next morning, they made way toward the place where Math son of Mathonwy and his host were. When they came, those men were going to take counsel which side they would await Pryderi and the men of the South. And they, too, came to the council. This is what they decided in their

Mochnant. The river Rhaeadr, which takes its name from the highest waterfall (Welsh *rhaeadr*) in Wales, flows southeast through the commot of Mochnant.

[65] Literally, 'Pig-stream' or 'Pig-vale.' In 1166 the commot of Mochnant in Powys was divided into Mochnant Uwch-Rhaeadr 'M. above the Falls' and Mochnant Is-Rhaeadr 'M. below the Falls.' This division later became the boundary between Denbighshire and Montgomeryshire.

[66] This Mochdre is just south of Colwyn Bay on the north coast.

[67] Creuwrion survives as 'Cororion' (in earlier records 'Crwrion' and 'Creweryon'), the name of a farm and a small lake near Tregarth. *Creu* (modern *crau*) means 'pigsty'; two references in early Welsh poetry suggest that *Gwrion* may be a variant of *Gwydion*. Though Cororion, at about 80-90 metres (245-275 feet) above sea level, is not a high as this passage seems to suggest, especially in a region that boasts peaks – though not towns – nearing 3,000 feet, there are nearby several remains of prehistoric settlement that the narrator may be referencing.

Mochdref (Mochdre). The town of Mochdre in the old cantref of Rhos, as seen from Bryn Euryn hillfort.

council – to wait in the fastness of Gwynedd in Arfon. And a stand was made in the midst of two districts, Maenor Bennardd and Maenor Coed Alun.

And Pryderi made toward them then, and there was the battle. And

Creuwrion. A farm and a small lake on the western border of Arllechwedd preserve the name Creuwrion in the modern form Cororion.

Nant Call (Nant Cyll). This stream flows into the Dwyfach about three miles southeast of Maenor Pennardd (Penarth), near the present village of Pant Glas.

great carnage was wrought on all sides, and it was necessary for the men of the South to retreat. This is where they retreated – as far as the place that is still called Nant Call, and they were pursued as far as there. And then there was slaughter of immeasurable extent. And then they retreated as far as the place called Dôl Benmaen. And then they came together and sought to make peace, and Pryderi gave hostages for the truce. This is whom he gave as hostage – Gwrgi Gwastra as one of twenty-four sons of noblemen.

And after that, they went on in their truce as far as Y Traeth Mawr. But since as soon as they came to Y Felenrhyd, the footsoldiers could not be restrained from shooting at each other, Pryderi sent messengers to ask for a prohibition on the two hosts, and to ask that it be left between him and Gwydion son of Dôn, since it was he who had caused that.

The messengers came to Math son of Mathonwy.

'Yea,' said Math, 'between me and God, if that pleases Gwydion son of Dôn, I will allow it gladly. I myself will not compel anyone to go to fight, instead of our doing what we are able.'

Y Traeth Mawr. Much of Y Traeth Mawr, 'The Great Beach,' was drained when a dike was built in the mid 19th century.

'God knows,' said the messengers, 'it would be fair, says Pryderi, for the man who did this wrong to him to pit his body against his own, and to let the two hosts be still.'

'To God I make my confession, I will not ask the men of Gwynedd to fight for me, but I myself will fight with Pryderi. I will pit my body against his gladly.'

And that was relayed to Pryderi.

'Yea,' said Pryderi, 'I will not ask anyone to claim my right except myself.'

Those men were set apart and their arming was begun, and they fought. And by force of power and craft, and magic and enchantment, Gwydion prevailed and Pryderi was slain. And in Maen Tyfiawg, above Y Felenrhyd, he was buried, and his grave is there.[68] The men of the South set out, with sad lamentation, toward their land. And that was no wonder – they had

[68] Maen Tyfiawg may be either a scribal error or a misunderstanding of the name Maentwrog, a village about a mile up the Dwyryd from Y Felenrhyd. The 9th- or 10th-century 'Stanzas of the Graves' state 'At the confluence of the Gwenoli / is the grave of Pryderi.'

Y Felenrhyd. The ford of Y Felenrhyd at the confluence of the Prysor and the Dwyryd, with Maentwrog (Maen Tyfiawg) in the middle distance.

The Gwenoli is a stream that flows into the Prysor just above Y Felenrhyd, about ³/₄ of a mile south-west of Maentwrog; see Thomas Jones, *The Black Book of Carmarthen 'Stanzas of the Graves'* (1967) p. 118–19.

lost their lord and many of their noblest men, and their horses and their arms for the most part.

The men of Gwynedd returned happy and exultant.

'Lord,' said Gwydion to Math, 'would it not be right for us to release their nobleman to the men of the South, whom they gave us as hostage for peace? And we ought not to imprison him.'

'Let him be freed,' said Math. And that

youth and the hostages who were with him were allowed to follow the men of the South.

Math himself made for Caer Dathyl. Gilfaethwy son of Dôn and the warband who had been with him went to make a circuit of Gwynedd as they had been accustomed, but without making for the court.

Math made for his chamber and he had a place prepared for him to recline, so that he could place his feet in the folds of the maiden's lap.

'Lord,' said Goewin, 'seek a maiden who may be beneath your feet now. I am a woman.'

'What is the meaning of that?'

'An attack, lord, was made upon me, and that openly, and I myself was not silent. There was none in the court who did not know of it. This is who came – your nephews, sons of your sister, lord, Gwydion son of Dôn and Gilfaethwy son of Dôn. And they did violence to me and shame to you, and I was slept with, and that in your chamber and in your bed.'

'Yea,' said he, 'that which I can, I will do. I will get compensation for you first, and afterward I myself will have my compensation. And you,' he said, 'I will take as my wife, and I will place the power of my realm in your hands.'

And at that they did not come in the vicinity of the court, but they remained on

Maen Tyfiawg
(Maentwrog).
The Maentwrog
standing stone,
which gave the
town its name,
now stands by
the wall of the
parish church.

Caer Dathyl.
An ancient stone
trackway leads to
the hillfort of Caer
Engan, another
possible location for
Caer Dathyl, about
two miles east of
Craig-y-Dinas.

the circuit of the land until a ban on food and drink for them went out. At first they did not come in his vicinity; then they came to him.

'Lord,' they said, 'good day to you.'

'Yea,' said he, 'is it to do right by me that you have come?'

'Lord, we are at your will.'

'If it had been my will, I would not have lost what I have lost of men and arms. My shame you cannot repay me for, not to mention the death of Pryderi. But since you came unto my will, I shall begin punishment upon you.'

And then he took his magic staff and struck Gilfaethwy so that he became a mature hind. And he seized the other swiftly – though he wished to escape, he was not able – and he struck him with the same magic staff so that he became a stag.

'Since you are bound together, I will make you go about together and be coupled, and in the same nature as the wild animals whose guise you are in. And at the time they have offspring, so shall you. And a year from today, come here to me.'

At the end of the year from that same day, behold he could hear a commotion under the wall of the chamber, and the barking of the dogs of the court above the commotion.

'See,' said he, 'what is outside.'

'Lord,' said one, 'I have looked. There is a stag and a hind there, and a fawn with them.'

And upon that, he arose and came out. And when he came, this is what he could see – the three creatures. This is the three creatures they were – a stag and a hind and a robust fawn. This is what he did – raised his magic staff.

'The one of you that was a hind last year, let him be a wild boar this year, and the one of you

[69] The names derive from *blaidd* 'wolf', *hydd* 'stag', and *hwch* 'swine'.

that was a stag last year, let him be a wild sow this year.' And upon that he struck them with his magic staff. 'The boy, however, I will take and I will have him reared and baptized.' (This is the name that he was given – Hyddwn.) 'You go, and let the one of you be as a wild boar and the other as a wild sow. And the nature the wild swine may have, let it be yours also. And a year from today you be here under the wall, and your offspring with you.'

At the end of the year, behold they could hear the barking of dogs under the wall of the chamber, and the gathering of the court above that in addition. Upon that he arose and went out. And when he came out, he could see three creatures. This is the sort of creatures he could see – a wild boar and a wild sow, and a goodly smallish creature with them, but it was stout for its age.

'Yea,' he said, 'this I will take to me, and I will have him baptized.' And he struck it with his magic staff so that it became a fair boy with thick auburn hair. This is the name that was given to that one – Hychdwn.

'And you, the one of you that was a wild boar last year, let him be a she-wolf this year, and the one that was a sow last year, let him be a wolf this year.' And upon that he struck them with his magic staff so that they were a wolf and a she-wolf. 'And the nature of the animals whose form you are in, let it be yours. And you be here a year from today under this wall.'

The same day at the end of the year, behold, he could hear a mustering and barking under the wall of the chamber. He went out, and when he came, behold, he could see a wolf and a she-wolf, and a strong wolf-cub with them.

'This I will take,' he said, 'and I will have him baptized. And his name is ready; this is it – Bleiddwn. Three sons are yours, and those three are:

Three sons of deceitful Gilfaethwy,
Three true champions,
Bleiddwn, Hyddwn, Hychdwn the Tall.'[69]

And upon that, he struck those two with the magic staff so that they were in their own flesh.

'Ah, men,' he said, 'if you have done wrong to me, long enough have you been punished, and great shame have you received, that a child has been born to each of you by the other. Have the men bathed and their heads washed, and have them clothed.'

And that was done for them. And after they had been arrayed, they went to him.

'Ah, men,' he said, 'you have obtained peace, and you shall have friendship. And give me counsel what maiden I should seek.'

Dylan. Maen Dylan, 'Dylan's Stone,' stands at the tip of the promontory of Bryn Arien (Trwyn Maen Dylan). Dinas Dinlle can be seen on the horizon to the left.

'Lord,' said Gwydion son of Dôn, 'counselling you is easy: Aranrhod daughter of Dôn, your niece, your sister's daughter.'[70]

She was brought to him. The maiden came in.

'Ah, maiden,' he said, 'are you a maiden?'

'I know not other than I am.'

Then he took the magic staff and bent it down.

'Step across this.' he said, 'and if you are a maiden, I shall know.'

Then she stepped across the magic staff, and with that step she left behind a large boy with thick yellow hair. This is what the boy did – he gave a loud cry. After the boy's cry, she made for the door, and upon that she left behind a small something. And before anyone could get a second glance at it, Gwydion took it, and wrapped a covering of silk brocade around it, and hid it. This is where he hid it – in a small chest at the foot of his bed.

'Yea,' said Math son of Mathonwy, 'I will have this one baptized,' referring to the yellow-haired boy. 'This is the name I will give – Dylan.'

The boy was baptized, and as soon as he was baptized he made for the sea. And on the spot, as soon as he came to the sea, he took the sea's nature, and he could swim as well as the best fish in the sea. And because of that he was called Dylan eil Ton. No wave ever broke beneath him.[71] And Gofannon, his uncle, struck the blow from which his death came, and that was one of the Three Unfortunate Blows.[72]

As Gwydion was one day in his bed waking up, he could hear a cry in the chest at his feet. Though it was not loud, it was loud enough that he heard it. This is what he did – he rose up quickly and opened the chest. And as he opened it, he could see a small boy tossing his arms about from the folds of the covering and scattering it. And he took the boy in his hands and he made for the town with him, where he knew there was a wet nurse. And he bargained with the woman to nurse the boy.

The boy was reared that year. And in the year's time, his stoutness would have been remarkable to them were he two years old. And the second year he was a large boy and able to set out for the court himself. Gwydion himself observed him keenly when he came to the court. And the boy grew intimate with him and loved him more than any other man. Then the boy

[70] A line in the *Book of Taliesin* describes her as 'Aranrhod famous for beauty greater than dawn in fair weather.' The first element of her name may be *Aran-*, as it appears throughout *The Mabinogi*, or *Arian-*, 'silver', found in other sources. *Aran*, possibly meaning 'round, humped' or 'huge', occurs in various place names in Wales, Scotland, and ancient Gaul. The second element is *-rhod* 'wheel'.

[71] The name may mean either 'Sea son (or grandson, descendant, or heir) of Wave,' or 'Sea like the Wave';

see note 37. Some have taken this passage to imply that Dylan became a fish, a selchie or man-seal, or other sea creature (see Sarah Keefer, 'The Lost Tale of Dylan' in C. W. Sullivan, ed., *The Mabinogi*, 79-97). However, this may just be the narrator's attempt at an etymological explanation of the name, and there may be some confusion with or play on the mythological name Dôn. The reference here to his death and other references in early poetry suggest that other tales were known about Dylan.

In the *Book of Taliesin*, we find a somewhat obscure 'Elegy to Dylan eil Ton,' and several additional references, including one naming him 'Dylan eil Môr.' (*Môr* is the common Welsh word for 'sea.') In the 'Stanzas of the Graves,' we find 'Where the wave makes a noise / the grave of Dylan [is] at Llan Beuno'; see Jones, '*Stanzas of the Graves*' (1967). On the shore about two-and-a-half miles north of the church of St. Beuno at Clynnog is a boulder known as Maen Dylan 'Dylan's Stone' near the hill referred to later in the tale as Bryn Arien.

[72] No other reference is known to this triad of Three Unfortunate Blows. This is not the same triad of Three Harmful Blows that is referenced at the end the Second Branch (see note 25). The latter uses *palfawd*, literally 'a slap with the palm'; the word used here is *ergyd*, a violent blow (with a fist or weapon). Gofannon was a mythological smith; he appears alongside Math in a poem in the *Red Book of Hergest*, and he is named Gofannon son of Dôn in the tale of *Culhwch and Olwen*.

was reared in the court until he was four years old. And it would be remarkable for a boy of eight to be as stout as he.

And one day he set out after Gwydion to walk about. This is what he did – he made for Caer Aranrhod, and the boy with him.[73] After he came to the court, Aranrhod rose up to welcome him and to greet him.

'May God prosper you,' he said.

'What boy is that behind you?' said she.

'This boy, he is your son,' he said.

'Alas, man! What has come over you to shame me, and to pursue my shame, and to keep it as long as this?'

'If there be upon you no greater shame than that I have raised a boy as good as this, a small thing will your shame be.'

'What is your boy's name?' she asked.

'God knows,' he said, 'he hasn't any name yet.'

'Yea,' she said, 'I will swear a destiny upon him, that he shall not have a name until I give it to him.'

'I confess to God,' he said, 'you are a wicked woman, but the boy shall have a name, though it be disagreeable to you. And you – ,' he said, 'because of this you are grieved, for you are not called a maiden. You will not ever again be called a maiden.'

And upon that he walked away in his anger and made for Caer Dathyl, and he was there that night. And the next day he arose and took his boy with him and went to walk about on the shore of the sea between there and Abermenai. And where he saw dulse and sea-girdle,[74] he made a ship by magic, and of the seaweed and dulse he made Cordovan leather, and plenty of that, and he stippled them so that no one had seen leather more fair than that.

And upon that he fitted a sail on the ship and came to the entrance of the gate of Caer Aranrhod, he and the boy, in the ship. And then he began to fashion shoes and sew them. And then they were observed from the fort. And when he knew that they were observed from the fort, he took away their own appearance and placed another appearance upon them, so they would not be recognized.

'What men are in the ship?' asked Aranrhod.

'Cobblers,' they said.

'Go to see what kind of leather they have and what kind of work they do.'

Then they came, and when they came, he was stippling Cordovan leather, and that was gilded. Then the messengers came and told that to her.

'Yea,' she said, 'take the measure of my foot and ask the cobbler to make shoes for me.'

He fashioned the shoes, though not according to the measure, but larger. The shoes came to her. Behold, the shoes were too large.

'These are too big,' she said. 'He shall have the value of these, but let him also make some that may be smaller than they.'

This is what he did – he made some others much smaller than her feet, and sent them to her.

'Tell him that not one of these shoes will go on me,' she said. It was told to him.

'Yea,' he said, 'I will not fashion shoes for her until I see her feet.' And that was told to her.

'Yea,' she said, 'I will go to him.'

And then she came to the ship. And when

[73] Caer Aranrhod or Caer Arianrhod, later corrupted to Tregaranthrag, is the name given to a line of rocks visible offshore only at extreme low tide, about a half mile south-west of Dinas Dinlleu.

[74] *Delysg* 'dulse' is a red or purplish edible seaweed. *Morwiail*, literally 'sea-rods,' is used for several varieties of brown seaweed, known in English variously as sea-girdle, oarweed, or wrack.

Caer Aranrhod
(Caer Arianrhod).
The rocks of Caer
Arianrhod are
visible only during
the lowest spring
tides of the year,
about a half mile
offshore between
Dinas Dinlle and
Trwyn Maen Dylan.

[75] *Llaw* 'hand,' *gyffes*
'skilled, skilful,' *lleu*
'bright, light, fair.'

[76] For this triad,
see note 48.

she came, he was fashioning and the boy was
sewing.

'Yea, lady,' he said, 'good day to you.'

'May God prosper you,' she said. 'It is
strange to me that you are not able to fit shoes
to measure.'

'I have not been able,' said he. 'I will be
able to do it now.'

And upon that, a wren lighted on the
gunwale of the ship. This is what the boy did –
he threw at it and struck it between the sinew
of its leg and the bone. This is what she did –
she laughed.

'God knows,' she said, 'it is with a skilful
hand the fair one hit it.'[75]

'Yea,' said he, 'God's curse on you. He has
got a name, and his name is good enough. He
is Lleu Llaw Gyffes from now on.'

And then the work vanished into dulse and
seaweed, and he pursued the work no farther
than that. And for that reason he was called
one of the Three Golden Shoemakers.[76]

'God knows,' said she, 'you will not be
better off for being disagreeable to me.'

'I have not been disagreeable to you yet,'
he said. And then he restored the boy to his
own appearance and took his own form.

'Yea,' said she, 'I will swear a destiny upon
this boy, that he shall not ever have arms until
I put them upon him.'

'Between me and God,' he said, 'this comes
from your wickedness, but he shall have arms.'

Then they came towards Dinas Dinlleu.
And then Lleu Llaw Gyffes was reared until he
was able to ride any horse, and until he was full-
grown in appearance and growth and size. And

then Gwydion recognized that he was becoming despondent for lack of horses and arms, and he called him to him.

'Ah, lad,' said he, 'we will go, you and I, on an errand tomorrow. Be more cheerful than you are.'

'And that I will do,' said the youth.

And next day, when the day was still young, they arose and took the seacoast up toward Bryn Arien. And at the highest point of Cefn Cludno they equipped themselves with horses and came toward Caer Aranrhod.[77] And then they altered their appearance and made for the gate in the guise of two young lads, except that Gwydion's appearance was graver than that of the boy.

'Porter,' he said, 'go in and say that bards from Morgannwg are here.' The porter went.

'God's welcome to them. Let them in,' she said.

They were met with very great joy. The hall was prepared and they went to eat. When they were done eating, she and Gwydion entertained themselves with stories and telling of tales. Gwydion himself was a good tale teller. After it was time for them to leave off the revelry, a chamber was prepared for them and they went to sleep.

At early cockcrow Gwydion arose, and then he summoned his magic and his power to him. By the time day was growing light, there was a bustling with trumpets and shouting throughout the land. When day was come, they heard knocking on the door of the chamber, and upon that Aranrhod asking them to arise. The young lad rose up and opened the door. She came in, and a maiden with her.

'Ah, nobles,' she said, 'we are in a bad situation.'

'Yea,' said he, 'we hear trumpets and shouting. What do you make of that?'

'God knows,' she said, 'we cannot get sight of the colour of the sea for all the ships pressed together, and they are making for land as swiftly as they can. What are we to do?' she asked.

'Lady,' said Gwydion, 'there is no counsel for us but to shut up the fort around us and to defend it as best we can.'

'Yea,' said she, 'May God repay you; you defend it, and here you will get enough arms.'

And upon that, she went after the arms, and lo, she came with two maidens with her and arms for two men with them.

'Lady,' he said, 'put arms upon this young man and I – the maidens and I – will put them upon myself. I hear the noise of the men coming.'

'I will do that gladly.' And she put arms upon him gladly and fully.

'Has the arming of that young man,' he asked, 'been completed?'

'It has been completed,' she said.

'Mine too is completed,' he said. 'Let us take off our arms now; we have no need of them.'

'Alas!' said she. 'Why? Behold the fleet around the house!'

'Ah, woman, there is no fleet there.'

'Alas,' said she, 'what sort of mustering was that?'

'A mustering,' said he, 'to break your destiny about your son, and to seek arms for him. And he has received arms – no thanks to you.'

'Between me and God,' said she, 'you are a wicked man, and many a boy might have lost

[77] Bryn Arien is a low promontory known locally as Trwyn Maen Dylan 'Dylan's Stone Nose'; see note 71 above. The location of Cefn Cludno is uncertain; Ifor Williams suggests the manuscript reading *clutno* should be emended to *clun tyno* and that Cefn Clun Tyno might thus be related to Coed Tyno (= 'Tyno Woods'), about a mile and a half south of Bryn Arien. On the highest point just above Coed Tyno are the remains of a prehistoric hill fort.

his life on account of the mustering you caused in this cantref today. And I will swear a destiny upon him,' she said, 'that he will not ever get a wife from the race that is now upon this earth.'

'Yea,' said he, 'you have always been a wicked woman, and no one ought to be a support for you. But he shall get a wife nonetheless.'

They came to Math son of Mathonwy, and they made the most persistent complaint in the world against Aranrhod and told how he had achieved all the arms for him.

'Yea,' said Math, 'let us seek, you and I, by our magic and enchantment, to conjure a woman for him from flowers.'

And he then had the stature of a man and was the most handsome youth a person ever saw. And then they took flowers of the oak and flowers of the broom and flowers of the meadow-sweet, and from those they produced by enchantment

Dinas Dinlleu
(Dinas Dinlle).
Looking south
across the ramparts
of Dinas Dinlle.

Mur Castell. The Roman walls of Mur Castell in Dunoding. The Norman mound (*tomen*) has given the site a new name, Tomen y Mur.

the fairest and most beautiful maiden a person ever saw, and baptized her with the baptism they used then, and gave her the name Blodeuedd.[78]

After they slept together at the feast, 'It is not easy,' said Gwydion, 'for a man without possessions to maintain himself.'

'Yea,' said Math, 'I will give him the single best cantref for a young man to have.'

'Lord,' he said, 'what cantref is that?'

'Cantref Dunoding,' he said. And that is now called Eifynydd and Ardudwy. This is where in the cantref he established his court – in the place which is called Mur Castell,[79] and that is in the uplands of Ardudwy, and there he established it and ruled over it. And everyone was content with him and his lordship.

[78] This name would have been understood as a double plural of *blodyn* 'flower,' thus, *blodau* 'flowers' with the additional early plural ending *-edd*.

Cynfael (Cynfal). The Cynfal flows swiftly west past Bryn Cyfergyd, just north of Mur Castell (Tomen y Mur).

79 Literally 'Castle Wall,' now known as (Castell) Tomen y Mur 'Mound of the Wall (Castle),' this is the site of a walled Roman fortification, with a small amphitheatre, built about 100 A.D. With spectacular views of the surrounding area, it protected a long stretch of the Roman road from Carmarthen to Caernarfon. The motte or mound built within the remains of the walls by William Rufus, the son of William the Conqueror, in the late 11th century may not have been there when *The Mabinogi* was composed.

78 In the *White Book* this name appears six times as *Gronw* and six as *Gronwy*; in contexts outside *The Mabinogi* his name is also given as *Goronw*(y) and *Grono*. The epithet *Pebr/Bebr/Befr* may derive from the adjective *pybr* 'strong,' or from *pefr* 'radiant, beautiful;' the latter appears in some versions of a triad related to this episode (see note 86 below). Penllyn is a cantref to the east of Ardudwy.

And then once upon a time he set out toward Caer Dathyl to visit with Math son of Mathonwy. The day he went toward Caer Dathyl, she took a turn within the court, and she could hear the call of a horn, and after the call of the horn, lo, a fatigued stag going past, with hounds and huntsmen after it. And after the hounds and the huntsmen, a band of men coming on foot.

'Send out a servant,' she said, 'to learn who the host is.'

The servant went and asked who they were.

'This is Gronw Bebr, the man who is lord of Penllyn,' they said.[80] The servant told that to her.

He chased after the stag, and on the River Cynfael he overtook the stag and killed it. And he was engaged in dressing the stag and feeding his hounds until night pressed upon him. And when the day was coming to an end and the night drawing near, he came past the gate of the court.

'God knows,' she said, 'we will be disgraced by the chieftain for letting him go at this hour to another country, if we do not invite him in.'

'God knows, lady,' they said, 'it is best to invite him in.'

Then messengers went up to him to invite him in. And then he received the invitation gladly and came to the court. And she came up to him to welcome him and to greet him.

'Lady, may God repay you your good cheer.' He removed his boots and they went to sit.

This is what Blodeuedd did – she looked at him. And the moment she looked, there was no part of her that was not full of love for him. And he gazed on her, and the same thought came to him as came to her. He could not hide that he loved her, and he told her so. She felt very great joy within her, and they talked that night about the love and the affection each one of them had placed on the other. And they did not delay their embracing beyond that night, and that night they slept together.

And the next day he asked leave to depart.

'God knows,' she said, 'do not go from me tonight.'

That night they were together also. And that night they took counsel together how they could get to be together.

'There is no counsel for you,' he said, 'but one: seek from him to learn how his death might come about, and that in the guise of care for him.'

The next day he asked to leave.

'God knows, I will not counsel you today to go from me.'

'God knows, since you do not counsel it, I will not go,' he said. 'I will say, however, there is a danger that the chieftain who owns the court will come home.'

'Yea,' she said, 'tomorrow I will let you leave.'

The next day he asked to leave, and she did not hinder him.

'Yea,' said he, 'remember what I have said to you and converse with him constantly, and that in the guise of a loving concern for him, but seek to learn from him what way his death might be brought about.'

He came home that night. They spent the day in conversing and song and revelry, and that night they went to sleep together. And he spoke to her, and a second time. And to that he got no response.

'What has happened to you?' he asked. 'Are you well?'

'I am thinking,' she said, 'that which you would not think about me. This is what it is –' she said, 'worrying about your death, if you were to go sooner than I.'

'Yea,' said he, 'may God repay you your care. Unless God kills me, however, killing me will not be easy,' he said.

'Will you, for God's sake and for my sake, tell me how you might be killed? Since my memory is better as a safeguard than yours.'

'I will gladly tell,' he said. 'It is not easy to kill me,' he said, 'with a blow. And there must be a year in making the spear I would be hit with, and without making any of it except when it would be during mass on Sunday.'

'Is that certain?' she asked.

'It is certain, God knows!' he said. 'My death cannot be accomplished inside a house,' he said; 'it cannot be accomplished outside. My death cannot be accomplished on horseback; it cannot be accomplished while I am on foot.'

'Yea,' said she, 'in what way could your death be accomplished?'

'I will tell you,' he said. 'By making a bath for me on the bank of a river and making an arched frame over the tub, and after that thatching it well and snugly too. And taking a goat buck,' he said, 'and placing it by the tub, and by me placing one foot on the back of the goat buck and the other on the edge of the tub. Whoever could strike me thus, he would bring about my death.'

'Yea,' said she, 'thank God for that! That can be avoided easily.'

No sooner had she had the explanation than she sent it to Gronw Bebr. Gronw laboured at the spear work, and the same day at the end of a year it was ready. And that day he let her know that.

'Lord,' she said, 'I am thinking how that could be which you told me earlier. Will you show me how you would stand on the edge of the tub and the goat buck, if I prepare the bath?'

'I will,' said he.

She sent to Gronw and asked him to be in the shadow of the hill that is now called Bryn Cyfergyr[81] – that was on the banks of the River Cynfael. What goats she had in the cantref she had rounded up, and brought them to the far side of the river, facing Bryn Cyfergyr.

And the next day she said, 'Lord,' she said, 'I have had the frame prepared, and the bath, and they are ready.'

'Yea,' said he, 'I will gladly go to look at them.'

They came next day to look at the bath.

'Will you go to the bath, lord?' she said.

'I will gladly,' he said.

He went to the bath and he bathed himself.

'Lord,' she said, 'lo, the animals which you said are called goat bucks.'

'Yea,' said he, 'have one of them caught and have it brought here.'

It was brought. Then he rose from the bath and put on his trousers, and he placed one foot on the edge of the tub and the other on the back of the goat buck.

Gronw rose up from the hill which is called Bryn Cyfergyr, and he rose on one knee, and with the poisoned spear he cast at him and struck him in his side, so that the shaft broke off from it, but the point remained in him. And then he flew up in the guise of an eagle and gave a horrible

Bryn Cyfergyr. This hill, now called Bryn Cyfergyd, rises sharply above the banks of the Cynfal.

[81] Literally, 'Hill of the Exchange of Blows.' This hill, now known as Bryn Cyfergyd, is about three miles to the north-east of Mur Castell.

Maenor Bennardd. This prehistoric cromlech in the Maenor Bennardd region stands near the farm now known as Penarth.

scream. And no sight of him was had from thenceforth. As swiftly as he went away, they made for the court and slept together that night.

And the next day Gronw arose and conquered Ardudwy. After conquering the country, he ruled it, so that Ardudwy and Penllyn were his.

Then the news came to Math son of Mathonwy. Math felt great sadness and care within him, and Gwydion more than he by far.

'Lord,' said Gwydion, 'I will not ever rest until I have news of my nephew.'

'Yea,' said Math, 'may God be your strength.'

And then he set out and began to wander about, and he wandered about Gwynedd and to the ends of Powys. After wandering everywhere, he came to Arfon, and he came to the house of a bondman in Maenor Bennardd. He dismounted at the house and remained there that night. The man of the house and his family came in, and last came the swineherd.

The man of the house said to the swineherd, 'Ah, lad,' he said, 'did your sow come in tonight?'

'Yes,' said he, 'just now she came to the pigs.'

'What sort of journey,' asked Gwydion, 'does that sow go on?'

'When the sty is opened every day, she goes out. None can keep hold of her, and it is not known what way she goes, any more than if she went into the earth.'

'Will you,' said Gwydion, 'for my sake, not open the sty until I am at the side of the sty with you?'

'I will gladly,' he said.

They went to sleep that night, and when the swineherd saw the light of day, he woke Gwydion. And Gwydion rose and dressed and came with him and stood by the sty. The swineherd opened the sty.

As soon as it was opened, lo, she leapt out and set off swiftly, and Gwydion followed her. And she headed upstream, and set out along a

82 It is not certain whether a late redactor of the tale composed these verses, inherited them from an earlier version, or adapted them from some other source; there are metrical irregularities in the original that may be the result of faulty transmission or copying, and the language of these verses is generally taken to be older than that of the tale. The 'two lakes' mentioned in the first line help to locate this episode geographically; the

Nantlleu. The Nantlle valley as viewed from the possible site of Dôl Bebin, the home of Goewin's father as mentioned at the beginning of the Fourth Branch.

sow went north-eastward from Maenor Bennardd up the river Llyfni to Dyffryn Nantlle (the Nantlle Valley), where there were two lakes. Though the lower one has since dried up, Llyn Nantlle Uchaf (Upper Nantlle Lake) remains, as does the name *Baladeulyn*, which means 'the place where the river flows from two lakes'. There is some evidence that one of these lakes may have been known as Llyn Gofannon; see note 72.

stream which is now called Nantlleu, and there she stayed and fed.

Gwydion came under the tree and looked to see what the sow was feeding on, and he could see that the sow was feeding on rotten meat and maggots. This is what he did – he looked in the top of the tree. And when he looked, he could see an eagle in the top of the tree. And when the eagle would shake itself, the vermin and the rotten meat would fall from it, and the sow was eating those things.

This is what he did – he thought that the eagle was Lleu, and he sang an *englyn*:[82]

An oak grows between two lakes,
Very dark are air and glen.
If I speak no lie,
This is because of Lleu's flowers.

This is what the eagle then did – he let himself down until he was in the middle of the tree.

This is what Gwydion then did – he sang another *englyn*:

An oak grows in a high plain.
Rain wets it not; no more heat melts it.
Nine score skills it supported.
In its top, Lleu Llaw Gyffes.

And then he let himself down until he was on the lowest branch of the tree.

He sang an *englyn* to him then:

An oak grows under a slope,
A comely lord's sanctuary.
If I speak no lie,
Lleu will come to my lap.

And he descended onto Gwydion's knee.

And then Gwydion struck him with the magic staff, so that he would be in his own guise. No one had ever seen a man looking more wretched, however, than he. He was nothing but skin and bone.

Then he made for Caer Dathyl, and there all the good physicians who could be found in Gwynedd were brought to him. Before the end of the year he was completely healthy.

'Lord,' he said to Math son of Mathonwy, 'it was high time for me to get compensation from the man from whom I took affliction.'

'God knows,' said Math, 'he cannot maintain himself with your compensation unpaid.'

'Yea,' said he, 'the sooner I may get compensation, the more pleasing to me.'

Then they mustered Gwynedd and made for Ardudwy. Gwydion set out in the lead, and he made for Mur Castell. This is what Blodeuedd did – she heard they were coming, took her maidens with her, and made for the mountain, and over the River Cynfael, making for a court that was on the mountain. But out of fear they did not know how to go except facing toward their back. And then they knew nothing until they fell into the lake, and they all drowned, except for her.[83]

Then Gwydion overtook her and said to her, 'I will not kill you; I will do what is worse to you. This is what that is –' he said, 'to let you go in the guise of a bird. And because of the shame you have done to Lleu Llaw Gyffes, you will not dare to show your face in the light

of day ever, and that out of fear of all the birds, and there will be enmity between you and all the birds, and it will be their nature to harass you and abuse you wherever they find you. And you shall not lose your name, but you will forever be called Blodeuwedd.'

This is what *blodeuwedd* is – 'owl' in the language of today. And for that reason the birds are hostile towards the owl, and the owl is still called *blodeuwedd*.[84]

Gronw Bebr made for Penllyn, and from there he sent a message. This is the message he sent – he asked Lleu Llaw Gyffes whether he wished for land or earth, or gold or silver for his insult-price.[85]

'To God I bring my confession, I will not take that,' he said. 'And here is the least thing I will take from him – that he go to the place where I was when he cast at me with the spear, and I in the place where he was, and let me cast at him with a spear. And that is the least thing I will take from him.'

---

[83] Though the narrator neglects to identify it explicitly, this episode is surely intended to explain the name of a small lake just over the ridge to the northeast of Mur Castell and Bryn Cyfergyr – *Llyn y Morynion* 'Lake of the Maidens.' Might it be that Blodeuedd and her maidens were following the Roman road north from Mur Castell that passes near Llyn y Morynion, perhaps hoping to reach safety at the site of a prehistoric settlement known now as Bryn y Castell?

[84] The narrator shifts the name *Blodeuedd*, a double plural as explained in note 78 above, to *Blodeuwedd*, from *blodau* 'flowers' + *(g)wedd* 'face, aspect, appearance,' an apt name for the owl—Flowerface.

[85] For the legal overtones of *ae tir ae daear* 'either land or earth,' see note 9.

[86] 'Three Faithless War-Bands of the Island of Britain:

The War-Band of Goronwy the Radiant of Penllyn, who refused to receive the poisoned spear from Lleu Skilful-Hand on behalf of their lord, at the Stone of Goronwy at the head of the Cynfal;

and the War-Band of Gwrgi and Peredur, who abandoned their lord at Caer Greu, when they had an appointment to fight the next day with Eda

---

The Lake of the Maidens. The small lake known as Llyn y Morynion, where Blodeuedd's maidens are said to have drowned, lies just east of the Roman road leading north from Mur Castell (Tomen y Mur).

That was told to Gronw Bebr.

'Yea,' said he, 'it is necessary for me to do that. My true noblemen and my warband and my foster brothers, is there any among you who will take the blow for me?'

'There is not, God knows,' they said.

And because they refused to suffer taking a single blow for their lord, they are called, from that day to today, one of the Three Unfaithful Warbands.[86]

'Yea,' he said, 'I will take it.'

And then those two came as far as the banks of the River Cynfael, and then Gronw Bebr stood in the place where Lleu Llaw Gyffes was when he cast at him, and Lleu in the place where he was.

And then Gronw Bebr said to Lleu, 'Lord,' he said, 'since it was through the cunning of a woman that I did to you what I did, I ask you, for God's sake, I see a stone slab on the bank of the river, let me place that between me and the blow.'

'God knows,' said Lleu, 'I will not refuse you that.'

'Yea,' he said, 'may God repay you.'

And then Gronw took the stone slab and placed it between him and the blow. And then Lleu cast at him with the spear, and he pierced through the stone slab and through him, too, so that his back was broken. And then Gronw Bebr was slain, and the stone slab is there on the bank of the River Cynfael in Ardudwy, with the hole through it. And because of that it is still called Gronw's Stone.[87]

Lleu Llaw Gyffes conquered the land a second time and ruled over it successfully. And as the tale says, he was lord over Gwynedd after that.[88]

and thus ends this branch of

THE MABINOGI

[87] Around 1990 a pierced stone about six feet in length was located on a small tributary of the Cynfael called Afon Bryn-saeth 'Arrow-hill River.' Found lying in a corner of a field known to the farmer as Bedd Gronw 'Gronw's Grave', this stone has recently been erected and set in concrete.

[88] A stanza from the 'Stanzas of the Graves' may refer to Lleu's story as told here, or to some other adventure: 'The grave of Lleu Llawgyffes under cover of the sea, / where his disgrace [or 'kinsman'] was, / a man who spared no one;' see Jones, *Stanzas of the Graves* (1967), 124-125.

Ceredigion
sunset.

Afterword

The Mabinogi in Its Medieval and Mythological Contexts

Anyone who has been in Wales will know how omnipresent are the reminders of history throughout the landscape. The window of the room in which I write this looks over a modern Welsh town with a nineteenth-century college, an eighteenth-century church, and the ruins of a thirteenth-century Anglo-Norman castle, and the backdrop to all this is an impressive Iron-Age hillfort. In such a setting one cannot help but think about the past at least once or twice during the day.

There must have been a similar effect at work in the eleventh century, before all but one of those structures were built, for there is no lack of Bronze-Age, Iron-Age, Roman, and post-Roman antiquities visible across the Welsh countryside. The eleventh-century inhabitants certainly pondered those remains when their original builders, their purpose, and their significance had been long forgotten. These early medieval residents also inherited traditions – names, stories, and cultural and historical references – from earlier generations. In many cases those traditions would provide explanations for the ancient artefacts around them, and these sites and places were incorporated into the local system of beliefs, traditions, and historical accounts. Thus, the very landscape became fertile ground for preserving and developing the cultural traditions that helped define the people who lived there.

The Mabinogi takes place in this specific and evocative setting, but in a vaguely defined time period – treiglgwaith 'once upon a time' (without the childish overtones that phrase has accumulated in English) – with no reference to the incursions of the Romans, the Anglo-Saxons, or the Normans, and a time, as well, that is essentially non-Christian, albeit not explicitly pre-Christian. For example, when Teyrnon finds the infant in the First Branch, the boy is baptized 'according to the baptism that was done then,' and the same is said of Blodeuedd in the Fourth Branch. The language and material culture of the tales, however, are not rigidly consistent with that setting. Characters wear silk brocade and cordovan leather, they make such exclamations as 'By my confession to God' and 'Oh, Son of God,' and Llwyd son of Cil Coed appears in the Third Branch disguised as a cleric, a priest, and a bishop. But rather than thinking of these seemingly anachronistic and Christian references as failures on the narrator's part, we can perhaps best understand them as ways in which the storyteller uses contemporary language and cultural references to convey the tonal subtleties of speech and to make the point of the narrative clear in terms familiar to his audience. Thus, Llwyd presents Manawydan – and us – with an easily recognizable hierarchy of increasing moral authority that needs no further explanation. Similarly, in the Fourth Branch, Lleu can only be killed with a spear that takes a year to make and that can only be worked on when people are at Mass on Sunday. This would surely signal to a medieval Christian audience the seriousness of the intended crime; even before the murder is attempted, the very act of making the spear puts the soul of its maker in jeopardy.

The medieval Welsh *cyfarwydd* (plural *cyfarwyddiaid*) had a role that was more significant than a modern reader might assume from such translations as 'tale teller' or 'storyteller.' The *cyfarwyddiaid* were not simply entertainers; they were responsible for preserving historical and genealogical information, along with cultural beliefs, traditions, and social ideals. In a preliterate society such lore can be best remembered and transmitted through poetry, tales, and other mnemonic resources such as the triads that are cited numerous times in *The Mabinogi* itself. We can be confident that the *writer* of *The Mabinogi*, insofar as we must consider it a written work, was successor to a long line of traditional oral storytellers, though we do not know the precise extent to which he may have revised, or restructured his source material. Thus, it is hard to place him at any specific point on a scale

ranging from scribe or copyist at one extreme to what we now think of as an author at the other. In any case, it is quite clear that *The Mabinogi* draws on traditions that are quite old, but not simply in order to preserve them for their own sake. The final storyteller has revitalized his sources, infusing them with a vision and a moral code relevant to the very real concerns of the contemporary medieval audience.

In order to understand *The Mabinogi* better, to be less puzzled than we might be, we must first and foremost set aside the all-too-common perception that people in the Middle Ages were less intelligent, less sophisticated, or less appreciative of the arts and literature than we are. Rather, we should recognise that the poets, artists, storytellers, and musicians of early medieval Wales, and their patrons and audiences, had a range of expectations, hopes, cares, and desires as complex and varied as our own, and that their works of art were created with great skill and purpose and are often imbued with both exquisite beauty and profound meaning. This recognition will help us to take *The Mabinogi* as seriously as we do more recent literary works.

But what is *The Mabinogi*? Is it one tale or four? It is clearly not a single tale in any simple sense, and although it seems that each of the four branches might stand alone, neither are they fully independent of each other. There are strong narrative links, for example, between the First and Third Branches, the First and Fourth Branches, and the Second and Third Branches, thus tying them all together.[1]

In order to see if there is an overall design to *The Mabinogi*, let us first consider the word *cainc*

[1] Much of the following discussion is drawn from two of my earlier articles, 'The Structure of *The Four Branches of the Mabinogi*' and 'The Role of Myth and Tradition in *The Four Branches of the Mabinogi*.' Both are reprinted in *The Mabinogi: A Book of Essays*, edited by C. W. Sullivan III (New York, 1996).

'branch,' which has several meanings that may be relevant to our understanding. The basic sense is 'a major branch of a tree,' as opposed to *brig*, the smaller twigs and branches, as attested in a passage in a medieval Welsh law text that may be considerably earlier than the thirteenth-century manuscript it appears in.[2] A second meaning of *cainc* is 'song, tune, or strain'. The earliest known example of this sense occurs six times in one of the satirical love laments of Dafydd ap Gwilym, the pre-eminent poet of Wales who died around 1380:

> I learned a song of paradise (*paradwysgainc*)
> With my hands at the end of a bench.
> …
> Here is the song (*cainc*) that on my bench…
> I composed, with the prod of love….[3]

This musical sense of *cainc* need not imply that the tales in *The Mabinogi* were originally sung; there is no evidence that they were ever narrated in verse. On the contrary, although the poets and storytellers in many early European cultures did sing their traditional and heroic tales, often to musical accompaniment, medieval Welsh tales are generally in prose, though they may contain some poetry in them. Thus, if we understand *cainc* in the sense of 'song or melody', it might be used not literally but metaphorically to convey something like the separate but related movements of a piece of music. A third possibly apt sense of *cainc* is 'a strand of rope.' Though the word *cainc* is not known in this sense before the late sixteenth century, it might suggest four tales woven or twisted together. Nevertheless, whichever sense we choose (my personal

preference is for the first), the underlying metaphor seems to indicate that each tale, each 'branch,' is one part of a larger whole.

The very fact that *The Mabinogi* is explicitly composed of four branches provides another important clue for our understanding, for this loose grouping helps us to avoid the temptation to try to find in the tales a linear continuum, a single story that might encompass the whole. Rather, the four branches are distinct but related and interconnected, much like – to introduce yet another metaphor – the complex interlace designs of early Celtic artwork and illuminated manuscripts such as the famous Book of Kells, the Lindisfarne Gospels, and the St. Chad Gospels, which were produced in the eighth century. In these works, decorative interlacing forms knots which then create a larger design or shape. So, too, with *The Mabinogi*; the four tales are juxtaposed in such a way that the reader might compare the events of one with another, while each forms a complete tale in itself. Thus, while any branch could potentially stand alone, both it and we would be much the poorer, for it would not then simultaneously illuminate and be illuminated by the others.

Like much early medieval narrative, *The Mabinogi* is told in a style that relies almost entirely on the description of events. We are told what happens and who says what, but we rarely learn what any character thinks or feels.[4] Nor does the narrator comment on the action or give us any insights into the psychology of the characters, as we have come to expect from the authors of modern novels. As with Biblical narrative, we must puzzle out the meaning of

[2] 'The value of a cross-branch [*trawsgainc*] which reaches the heart of a tree, thirty pence; beyond that, it is a bough [*brig*] and has no legal value;' Dafydd Jenkins, *The Law of Hywel Dda* (Gomer, 1986), 188.

[3] Translated from Thomas Parry, *Gwaith Dafydd ap Gwilym* (Caerdydd, 1963), 375.

[4] Thus, on those few occasions when we do get an indication of a character's thoughts, we should pay particularly close attention.

the text ourselves, though there are numerous signposts to guide us along the way.

The most obvious of such guides are the explicit narrative links between the branches and between episodes of each branch. For example, the gifts that Pwyll receives from Annwn in the First Branch provide an excuse for starting a war in the Fourth Branch; revenge for Pwyll's treatment of Gwawl in the First Branch is exacted in the Third Branch; and the expedition to Ireland in the Second Branch results in the usurpation of Manawydan which is redressed in the Third Branch. These links are not trivial or fortuitous; they account for the motivations of characters and episodes in important ways.

In addition to these narrative or structural links between branches, there are also thematic links that convey the meaning or implications of the narrative. Often these are most easily discerned through the comparison of similar events. The author, it seems clear, expects the audience to keep various themes in mind, and often a slight reference or a similarity in wording will connect episodes implicitly, so that we are reminded of an earlier one as we read another.

In a broad sense, *The Mabinogi* is a study in how to behave, and as such it must have served, in part, as an entertaining set of *exempla*, cautionary tales, or guidelines for the aristocratic patrons and audience who supported the *cyfarwyddiaid*, the traditional storytellers, and who paid considerable sums to have the tales written down. The persistent concern of the narrator of *The Mabinogi* is the ways in which personal behaviour binds society together – or pulls it apart. Failure to behave according to

social standards of right and wrong leads inevitably, in these tales at least, to discord and shame, or even war and death. But the narrator is not overtly dogmatic; not telling us what is right or wrong, but simply telling the story, leaving it to us to discern the themes and the meaning behind
them. *Dealled y darlleawdr*, as says the tag to some fables translated from Latin into Welsh in the fourteenth century: Let the reader understand.[5]

Three important themes, which can be classified under the headings of Friendships, Marriages, and Feuds, account for much of the action of *The Mabinogi*. These appear in each branch, and the variation among them gives us multiple perspectives from which to consider their significance. Tracing these themes through *The Mabinogi* helps reveal the underlying pattern of the whole and teaches us much about human nature in the process. While we cannot here follow them in all their detail, we can perhaps illustrate how to discern the inherent themes by tracing a few examples.

The word 'friendship' (*cydymdeithas*) occurs fifteen times in *The Mabinogi*, no fewer than eight of them within the first five pages of this translation. Thus there can be little doubt that friendship is important in the opening episodes of the First Branch. Pwyll seeks to make amends for laying claim to Arawn's stag by stating, "...if I have done wrong, I will purchase your friendship" (p. 21). The conversation then establishes how Pwyll can gain Arawn's friendship – explicitly by fighting in Arawn's stead in single combat. Arawn magically shifts Pwyll into his own shape, suggesting he can even

5 Ifor Williams, *Chwedleu Odo* (Caerdydd, 1957), 13, 18, 23.

sleep with his own (Arawn's) wife. This is surely an implicit test of Pwyll's character, similar to the bedroom temptation of Gawain in the fourteenth-century English poem *Sir Gawain and the Green Knight*.[6] But unlike Gawain, Pwyll goes far beyond what was required of him throughout the entire year. As Arawn's wife puts it to her husband afterward, '"...a strong hold you had on a friend in regard to fighting with the temptation of the flesh and keeping faith with you"' (p. 24). Upon his return, Pwyll's men, too, recognise the importance of these events and his new bond with the king of Annwn: '"Yea, lord," they said, "thank God you have got that friendship"' (p. 24). This section of the First Branch closes with a clear reiteration of the continuing bond between Pwyll and Arawn: 'And from then on they began to strengthen the friendship between them and to send each other horses and hounds and hawks and every kind of jewel which each one supposed would please the thought of the other' (p. 24).

Let us jump ahead now to the Fourth Branch. Gwydion seeks to foment a war to get Math away from his footholder, and we are reminded of the friendship between Pwyll and Arawn when Gwydion identifies the swine that he says he will get from Pryderi, Pwyll's son: 'They were sent to him from Annwn by Arawn King of Annwn' (p. 80). This is important not merely to explain the origin of the swine – the narrative link – but to recall the friendship – the thematic link – because events in the Fourth Branch, we later learn, hinge on the friendship between Math and Pryderi. The generosity and trusting nature of Pryderi are contrasted with the magic, cunning, and trickery of Gwydion before and during their combat, but the full implications of Pryderi's death become clear only after Math returns from the war and finds that his footholder has been raped. Math rebukes Gwydion and Gilfaethwy, "If it had been my will, I would not have lost what I have lost of men and arms. My shame you cannot repay me for, not to mention the death of Pryderi" (p. 91). Only then does the import of events strike home; Math has been tragically deprived of a friend and was even instrumental in his death.

Why, then, did Math go so quickly to war against Pryderi in the first place? The answer lies in the fact that Gwydion and Gilfaethwy are his nephews, his sister's sons. This is one of the closest relationships in much of early medieval European culture and literature. When Gwydion is pursued by Pryderi, the blood tie proves stronger than that of friendship, and thus the men of Gwynedd are gathered against those of the South. This brings to mind, in turn, similar family ties noted at the beginning of the Second Branch. Bendigeidfran can not take revenge against the easily offended Efnisien, who has insulted Matholwch: '"And tell him what kind of man did that, and that it is against my own will that that was done, and that it is a brother with the same mother as I who did that, and it is not easy for me either to kill him or to destroy him"' (p. 47). All Bendigeidfran can do to compensate for the injury is offer the insult price legally due to a king, with added recompense in the form of the cauldron. However, in spite of his generosity and the fact that the matter has been legally resolved, the insult festers for two

[6] There are several other similarities between this famous Middle English poem and the story of Pwyll.

years among the men of Ireland, with disastrous results when the feud is later renewed.

Another important friendship is woven into the last part of the First Branch. Teyrnon has mysteriously found a child who turns out to be Pwyll's son. The narrator stresses the bond of friendship that develops after Teyrnon unselfishly restores the boy to his rightful parents: '"Between me and God," declared Pwyll, "while I live I will maintain you, both you and your realm, as long as I can maintain my own. If he lives, it is better for him to maintain you than for me"' (p. 38–39). This relationship, in which Teyrnon acts honourably even though he and his wife had hoped to keep the boy, serves as a model of friendship and loyal behaviour in comparison with others that result in feud and war.

The Third Branch contains the most extended examination of friendship in *The Mabinogi*. The relationship of Pryderi and Manawydan provides the motivation for much of the action and serves as a focal point of the tale. The branch opens with the formation of a strong friendship between them, set in the context of Caswallawn's usurpation of Manawydan's rule. By offering the seven cantrefs of Dyfed to Manawydan, Pryderi prevents the likely outbreak of a potentially disastrous feud between Caswallawn and Manawydan. As we think back to the story of Caswallawn's treachery and the death of Cradawg recounted in the Second Branch, we are reminded of the reference there to the triad of the 'Three People who Broke their Hearts from Bewilderment' (p. 58), which links the death of Cradawg with the tragic death of Branwen, also the result of a feud which should not have been

renewed. The friendship between Pryderi and Manawydan is made explicit when Manawydan says, '"May God repay you your friendship,"' and Pryderi replies, '"The best friendship I can give will be yours, if you wish it"' (p. 63). This is emphasized again after Manawydan meets Rhiannon: '"And may God repay the man who is granting to me his friendship as steadfast as that"' (p. 64). And indeed, a strong friendship is established among the four companions: 'And upon that a friendship grew among those four so that not one of them wished to be without the other either day or night' (p. 65).

With Manawydan under his care, Pryderi then tenders his homage to Caswallawn, thus ensuring that all those in his realm, including Manawydan, will remain peaceful. After the enchantment falls on Dyfed, the author repeatedly compares and balances the actions of Manawydan and Pryderi in their efforts to survive during the enchantment on Dyfed. During their time as craftsmen in Lloegr (England), the dynamics of the relationship seem to be reversed, and it is Manawydan who counsels restraint in response to Pryderi's anger and his wish to '"kill those churls." "No," he replied, "Caswallawn would hear of that, and his men, and we would be ruined"' (p. 67).

Manawydan provides the advice and skills by which they survive, but when Pryderi disappears into the mysterious fort, we, like Rhiannon, are led to doubt his judgement:

'Where,' she said, 'is your friend, and your hounds?'

'Here,' he answered, 'is my tale,' and he related it all.

'God knows,' said Rhiannon, 'a bad friend have you been, and a good friend have you lost.' (p. 70)

In effect, Rhiannon implies that Manawydan should have gone into the fort to try to rescue Pryderi (or perhaps to die trying), as she then sets out to do, only to be caught herself and the two are spirited away.

This leaves us questioning Manawydan's behaviour or his bravery, as the tale moves away from the imprisonment of Pryderi and Rhiannon to focus on the relationship between Manawydan and Cigfa, Pryderi's wife. In order to allay Cigfa's fear of being left alone with him, Manawydan delivers a strong, even repetitive, affirmation of his friendship and loyalty to Pryderi and to her: '"Between me and God, though I were in the spring of my youth, I would keep trust with Pryderi, and for your sake I would keep it. And let there be not a single fear upon you," he said. "Between me and God," he said, "you shall have the friendship you wish from me, to the best of my ability, while God may see fit for us to be in this wretchedness and care"' (p. 70–1). As the two return to Lloegr, Cigfa shows concern about his behaviour and his status when he decides to take up shoemaking again: '"Lord," she said, "that is not acceptable in its cleanliness for a man of such skill, of such rank as you"' (p. 72).

Later our doubts increase considerably when Manawydan apparently becomes obsessive in his determination to hang the mouse he has caught stealing his grain. As Rhiannon earlier implied, it seems that Manawydan has not been acting as a nobleman is expected to act. Cigfa, too, says,

'"…it is unpleasant to see a man of such rank, of such nobility as you hanging that sort of creature"' (p. 73). At this point the reader is inclined to agree with the assessment of these two women. Not until after the cleric, priest, and bishop are revealed to have been Llwyd son of Cil Coed and the cause of the enchantment is finally made known, do we realize that Manawydan has had much more understanding than the others – or us. In retrospect we can see that his prudent counsel all along has been aimed at removing the enchantment from Dyfed, restoring Pryderi and Rhiannon to freedom, and ensuring future peace and order. This prudence may be one of Manawydan's traits in earlier Welsh tradition; he is listed, for instance, in a tenth- or eleventh-century poem cataloguing Arthur's heroes: 'Manawydan son of Llŷr, / profound was his counsel.'[7]

The final episode of the Third Branch not only ties up the narrative strands, it shows how the themes of Friendship, Marriage, and Feud link this tale with the others, for as the marriage of Rhiannon and Manawydan establishes the initial peace as well as the friendship, at the end we have the resolution of a feud which carried over from one generation to the next. In this tale we can see especially clearly how the author balances these themes and carefully controls the dramatic elements, resolving loose ends only at the last moment, making clear the significance of what had seemed perplexing or irrelevant.

It is striking that there is at least one marriage in each of the four branches. The relationship of Pwyll and Rhiannon takes up much of the First Branch. Events at the two wedding feasts

[7] This poem from *The Black Book of Carmarthen* is translated in John K. Bollard, 'Arthur in the Early Welsh Tradition,' *The Romance of Arthur*, edited by James J. Wilhelm (New York, 1994), 17-18.

at the court of Hefeydd the Old reveal much about Pwyll's character traits, and we later learn that they also provide the motivation for events in the Third Branch – Gwawl's complaint against Pwyll. In both the First and Second Branches we have a theme that became quite popular in the Middle Ages, the theme of the Calumniated Wife or the wife wrongly accused,[8] and there is a marked contrast in the response of the two husbands in these tales. Whereas Pwyll learns to weigh carefully his own words and the advice he receives, Matholwch repeatedly – and disastrously – concedes to the flawed advice of his foster brothers and counsellors. Indeed, counsel can be seen as another persistent theme running throughout *The Mabinogi*, for the terms 'counsel' or 'council' appear frequently throughout the text, especially in the Second Branch.

In the Third Branch marriage functions both as a means of maintaining peace, as with Pryderi's offer of Rhiannon to Manawydan, and as establishing further obligations of friendship, exemplified in Manawydan's reassurance regarding his intentions toward Cigfa when he is left alone with her. This unusual situation, in which a man and a woman live together though each is married to someone else, must have been understood then as now as a fairly direct expression of the vulnerability of women in a world controlled by men.

Many of the events in the Fourth Branch are driven by an excess of sexual passion. In the first part of the tale, Gilfaethwy's love for Goewin leads to violent rape – the explicit expression of the vulnerability of women, especially during war. Math's response to this crime is remarkable not

only for the ignominious punishment he imposes on Gilfaethwy and Gwydion, i.e. for each to engender offspring on the other – but also for the recompense he offers to Goewin: '"And you," he said, "I will take as my wife, and I will place the power of my realm in your hands"' (p. 90). Never before or since, I suspect, has a rape victim been responded to with such magnanimity, proffered without hesitation. This is in stark contrast not only with the mistreatment of Branwen in the Second Branch, but also with the faithlessness of Blodeuedd, who plots with her lover to kill her husband in the latter part of the Fourth Branch.

The friendships and marriages in *The Mabinogi* are woven into a tapestry of antagonisms, feuds, and wars, potential or realized, which can be catalogued in a set of paired names: Pwyll-Arawn, Arawn-Hafgan, Pwyll-Gwawl, Efnisien-Matholwch, Bendigeidfran-Matholwch, Pryderi-Llwyd, Math-Pryderi, Gwydion-Aranrhod, Lleu-Gronw. An examination and comparison of the causes, resolutions, and effects of these feuds further illuminates the worldview that the narrator of *The Mabinogi* propounds, a view based on a deep understanding of human nature and one that offers ways to think and act beyond the traditional heroic code of loyalty, warfare, and revenge. We are shown, from varying perspectives, the disastrous effects of rash actions and words, the more positive results of prudence and respect for the bonds of kinship and friendship, and the value of trust and a straightforward honesty. If even today we could take to heart the lessons of *The Mabinogi*, we might be more at peace.

[8] A classic example is found in the Man of Law's Tale in Geoffrey Chaucer's *Canterbury Tales*.

The Mythological Background

While a number of the characters and events in *The Mabinogi* clearly derive from pre-Christian Celtic mythology, that mythology is shadowy at best, discernible primarily through the lens of comparative analysis and the work of scholars. The medieval Christian storytellers, scribes, and their patrons would have little or no conscious interest in preserving what they would consider pagan beliefs and lore, certainly not without some sort of disclaimer as we find in one version of the *Táin Bó Cúalgne*, one of the great Irish mythological narratives:

> *I who have copied down this story, or more accurately fantasy, do not credit the details of the story, or fantasy. Some things in it are devilish lies, and some poetical figments; some seem possible and others not; some are for the enjoyment of idiots.*[9]

However, tales that are significant within a culture, carrying moral lessons or other messages of social value, continue to be told over generations. Themes may be recast and adapted to changing beliefs, conditions, and tastes, and as one religion is supplanted by another the tales no longer function as primary mythology, though some of the underlying mythological lore remains with them as they are passed along. While such remains in *The Mabinogi* are insufficient for reconstructing with confidence a pre-Christian Welsh or British Celtic mythology, they do shed some light on the little that is known about early Celtic beliefs in Britain. The clearest indications of the mythological background of *The Mabinogi* are found in the names and attributes of various characters, the most significant of whom are discussed below.

The name Rhiannon derives from a Celtic form *Rigantona* 'divine queen.' (The masculine ending *–onos* and the feminine *–ona* denote divine status). There is no known early reference to a goddess Rigantona, but given the various equine connections of Rhiannon, many scholars have proposed that she may originally have been the same figure as *Epona*, the Celtic horse goddess who was venerated throughout Celtic Europe and even in North Africa and Rome itself.[10] Rhiannon first appears riding a magical horse; the birth and boyhood of her son is intertwined with the birth of a foal under mysterious, if not supernatural, circumstances; her punishment is to sit on a mounting block and to offer to carry visitors to the court on her back, i.e. to take on the role of a horse, and she wears a collar or yoke during her captivity. Other aspects of her character, especially the possession of a magical bag that cannot be filled, also suggest her divine origins.

Though he is a relatively minor character in the First Branch, Teyrnon can be linked, etymologically at least, with Rhiannon, for his name is the masculine equivalent of hers. Teyrnon derives from *Tigernonos* 'divine king.' That he is a character of exemplary goodness and loyalty may reflect his origins as a beneficent early Celtic deity.

Many of the attributes of Bendigeidfran, Brân Fendigaid (Brân the Blessed), or simply Brân, as his name appears in various sources, suggest that he is of divine origin. *Brân* is Welsh for 'crow, raven,' and the raven is associated with a number

[9] Translated by Thomas Kinsella, *The Táin* (Oxford, 1970), p. 238.

[10] See *The Horse in Celtic Culture*, edited by Sioned Davies and Nerys Ann Jones (Cardiff, 1997), pp. 11-14, 168-173.

of Celtic deities and heroes, especially in the context of war, such as the Irish goddesses known as the Badbh and the Morrigán, both of whom could take the form of ravens. Bendigeidfran is of giant stature; he possesses a cauldron of rebirth; his death is brought about only through the wound of a poisoned spear in the foot (not unlike Achilles and Krishna); and he has the power to stave off – for a time at least – the finality of death. The burial of his head in London and the reference to the triads of the Three Fortunate Concealments and Three Unfortunate Disclosures are possibly reflections of an earlier practice of talismanic burial to protect a territory. Certainly the human head was important in early Celtic belief and ritual.

Manawydan son of Llŷr has been equated with Manannán mac Lir, the Irish god of the sea and a master of wisdom, crafts, and magic, and both names are related to the territorial name *Manaw*, the early Welsh name for the Isle of Man, also occurring in *Manaw Gododdin*, a region in what is now southern Scotland and whose heroes are eulogized in the Early Middle Welsh poem known as *The Gododdin*. The Welsh *llŷr* means 'sea,' but unlike Manannán there is no other evidence that either Manawydan or Llŷr were sea divinities in Welsh tradition. It is likely that the medieval Welsh poets and storytellers understood a short form of his name, Manawyd, to refer to Manawydan's skill in leather crafts, for *manawyd* is the Welsh word for 'awl.'

Both the name Lleu and the epithet Llaw Gyffes 'Skilful Hand' are paralleled in those of the Irish god Lugh Samildánach 'Lugh Skilled-in-many-arts.' Lleu and Lugh are cognate with the Gaulish *Lugus*, whose name is preserved in those of several western European cities, including Lyons, Laon, Leiden, and Luguvalium, the Latin name for Carlisle in Scotland. Lugus was clearly an important Celtic deity, and he is probably the god that Caesar calls Mercury when he states, 'The god they [the Gauls] reverence most is Mercury. They have very many images of him and regard him as the inventor of all the arts.'[11]

Gwydion and Aranrhod, the children of Dôn, have important mythological and divine origins, for their mother can be equated etymologically with Danu, the mother of the Irish gods, the Tuatha Dé Danann 'the people of the goddess Danu,' and of the Indo-European goddess Dānu in the early Sanskrit *Rig Veda*, whose name, which means 'stream,' survives in the rivers Don, Dnieper, and Danube.[12] Gofannon, another son of Dôn, and the uncle and slayer of Dylan Eil Ton, is a mythological blacksmith (*gof*), who also appears briefly in the early Welsh Arthurian tale of *Culhwch and Olwen*. Both his name and his character match the Irish Goibhniu, the divine smith who forges unfailing weapons for Lugh and the Tuatha Dé Danann.

Not only characters, but events and references in *The Mabinogi* also indicate a Celtic mythological origin. Most striking, perhaps is the cauldron of rebirth in the Second Branch. Cauldrons were of great ritual significance as well as practical use in early Celtic society, and the cauldron of rebirth itself has parallels in Irish mythology and literature and also in a broader Celtic context. The famous silver-gilt Gundestrup cauldron, made perhaps in Gaul or perhaps in Romania or Thrace in the first or second century BCE, and found buried in a

[11] *The Conquest of Gaul*, translated by S. A. Handford, (Harmondsworth, 1951), p. 33. A Latin inscription from Osma, Spain, reveals a connection between the Lugoves (plurul of *Lugus*) and shoemaking: *Lugovitus Sucrum L. L. Urico collegio sutorum d[ono] d[edit]*,' L. L. Urico donated this, sacred to the Lugoves, to the guild of shoemakers'. (Translated and discussed by W. J. Gruffudd, *Math Vab Mathonwy* [1928], pp. 237-8).

[12] See Alwyn and Brinley Rees, *Celtic Heritage* (London, 1961), pp. 52-53.

Danish marsh, has a panel depicting a large figure, who may be a god, accompanied by soldiers and holding a man over a cauldron, perhaps in the act of resurrecting him. In 'The Spoils of Annwn,' a somewhat obscure tenth-century Welsh poem in the *Book of Taliesin*, we hear of an overseas raid made by Arthur and his men on a magical fortress known 'according to the story of Pwyll and Pryderi.' The poet speaks of 'the cauldron of the Head of Annwn…/ It does not boil a coward's food,' and tells us that from this raid, as in the expedition to Ireland in the Second Branch, 'except for seven, none returned.'[13] This poem, along with others in the same manuscript, strongly suggests the existence of a different version or versions of at least some episodes in *The Mabinogi*.

Some elements of *The Mabinogi* have a resonance even deeper than Celtic mythology *per se*. For example, Lleu, it seems, is invulnerable not only because he must be killed with a spear produced during sacred time over the course of a year, but also because he can not be killed on land or on water, nor inside or outside a house, nor on foot or on horseback – hence the goat and the tub on a river bank under a thatched frame. This complex set of contradictory requirements to bring about a character's death is closely matched by the story of the slaughter of Hiranya Kashipu ('Golden Clothes') by Narasimha ('Man-lion'), well known in ancient Indian tradition.[14] This is, therefore, a very old Indo-European motif, and as Kenneth Jackson shows, it appears in many European folktales later than these Sanskrit and Welsh sources, though usually in a riddling context rather than as the necessary conditions for someone's death.[15]

The Manuscripts

The Mabinogi has survived complete in two medieval manuscripts, along with two fragments from a third manuscript. The present translation is based primarily on the earliest complete manuscript, the *White Book of Rhydderch*, which was written in the mid-fourteenth century, probably (in part at least) at the Cistercian abbey of Strata Florida, and which was, in all likelihood, commissioned and owned by Rhydderch ab Ieuan Llwyd (c.1325–c.1398), a county official, an expert in Welsh law, a literary patron, and a descendant of the Lord Rhys, who died in 1197, the last and the greatest Welsh ruler of Deheubarth (south-west Wales). The manuscript, now bound in two parts, is held by the National Library of Wales under the designation NLW Peniarth 4 and 5. The *White Book* is a not an elegant manuscript, but it contains an important anthology of Welsh prose tales, translations from French romance, and other traditional Welsh material, including a copy of many of the *Triads of the Island of Britain* and of early Welsh poetry that was already archaic, some of which deals with traditional characters who appear in various of the narratives. A number of primarily religious texts translated into Welsh were later bound with this collection.[16]

The other complete text of *The Mabinogi* is found in the *Red Book of Hergest*, now MS Oxford, Jesus College 111, in the Bodleian Library at Oxford. This massive collection of medieval Welsh poetry, historical prose, and prose narratives was written for Hopcyn ap Tomas ab Einion soon after 1382 by a professional scribe

[13] The full text is translated in John K. Bollard, 'Arthur in the Early Welsh Tradition,' in *The Romance of Arthur*, edited by James J. Wilhelm (New York, 1994).

[14] An elaborate version of this motif is found in the 9th-century Sanskrit *Bhāgavata Purāna* (Book VII, Chapters 1-10). Note too that Lleu stands 'in the shadow of the hill,' i.e. neither in light nor darkness, that he bathes beforehand, and is only partially dressed when he is struck. These further conditions are paralleled in the 14th century Sanskrit tale of Rohaka; see Kenneth Jackson, *The International Popular Tale and Early Welsh Tradition*, p. 110.

[15] See Kenneth Jackson, *The International Popular Tale and Early Welsh Tradition*, pp. 109-113.

[16] For a detailed examination of the manuscript, see Daniel Huws, 'Llyfr Gwyn Rhydderch,' in *Medieval Welsh Manuscripts* (Cardiff, 2000), pp. 227-268.

named Hywel Fychan. In addition to *The Mabinogi*, the *Red Book* contains six other Welsh tales also found in the *White Book*. These are *Culhwch and Olwen* (the earliest Welsh Arthurian tale), *Maxen Wledig* (a story of how the emperor of Rome found a Welsh wife, whose brothers then helped him regain his throne), *Lludd and Llefelys* (a folktale of three strange and magical plagues overcome by the king of Britain and his brother), and three Arthurian tales, *Peredur, Owain,* and *Geraint.* It has long been suggested that a seventh tale in the *Red Book, The Dream of Rhonabwy* (a tongue-in-cheek satire on Arthurian narrative style), may have been in a missing portion of the *White Book,* but there is no actual evidence that it was. When these tales began to attract attention in the early nineteenth century, they were translated and published by Lady Charlotte Guest between 1838 and 1849 under the title *The Mabinogion,* a title which, as explained below, is a misnomer based on an error, but which has proved so popular that it is still in use.

The earliest known fragments of *The Mabinogi* are two leaves from a manuscript written in the second half of the thirteenth century and now included in NLW Peniarth 6. One leaf contains a passage from the Second Branch and the other a passage from the Third Branch. The importance of these short fragments is not only that they demonstrate the existence of *The Mabinogi* some generations earlier than the *White Book,* but that their language and spelling provide evidence that they were copied from an even earlier source and that *The Mabinogi* seems to have been in something very like its present state by the late eleventh century.[17]

17 In his detailed examination of the evidence for establishing a date for *The Mabinogi*, T. M. Charles-Edwards concludes, 'It is, therefore, likely that the Four Branches belong to sometime between about 1050 and about 1120,' 'The Date of the Four Branches of the Mabinogi,' in *The Mabinogi: A Book of Essays*, edited by C. W. Sullivan III (New York, 1996), p. 53.

The Title

As in many medieval manuscripts, there are no titles at the beginning of the texts in the *White Book of Rhydderch.* Rather, each of the four branches begins with a large red initial and ends with the statement 'And thus ends this branch of *The Mabinogi*' or a variation of it. As it happens, at the end of the First Branch the manuscript reads *mabynnogyon.* The form *mabinogion,* to use the Modern Welsh spelling, does not appear elsewhere in early Welsh, and it is generally accepted that it is an example of a well-known type of scribal error in which part of a preceding word is inadvertently recopied. Just above this word in the manuscript we find *dyledogyon* 'nobles, noblemen', from *dyledog* 'nobleman' plus the common plural ending –*yon*, modern –*ion*. The reading *mabynnogyon* in the First Branch can thus be confidently corrected to *mabynnogi* or *mabinogi,* as found in the remaining three branches. (Understanding *mabinogion* as a plural led the eighteenth-century scholar William Owen Pughe, followed later by Lady Guest and her editors, to adopt it as the title for what they defined as a collection of tales, though these tales do not appear as a unified collection either in the *White Book* or in the *Red Book* from which Guest took them.)

The question naturally arises: What does *mabinogi* mean? Unfortunately, we have no simple answer. The ultimate root of the word *mabinogi* is undoubtedly *mab* 'boy, son'. Thus many nineteenth- and early twentieth-century scholars came to understand *mabinogi* to mean a tale of the birth and youth of a hero. This interpretation has the support of the title given to one copy of the medieval Welsh translation of the Latin Apocryphal Gospel *De Infantia Jesu Christi*, which recounts the childhood (*infantia*) of Jesus: *llyma vabinogi Iesu Grist*, 'Here is the *mabinogi* of Jesus Christ'. This, combined with the use of the term by the early thirteenth-century poet Prydydd y Moch in reference to the youth of the prince Llywelyn ab Iorwerth, suggests that medieval Welsh audiences may have similarly understood the word.

Alternatively, Professor Eric Hamp has cogently argued on linguistic evidence that *mabinogi* derives from the name of the Celtic god Maponos ('the Divine Son'), son of Matrona ('the Divine Mother'), whose name in Welsh becomes Mabon ap Modron. Hamp argues that in its original form *The Mabinogi* recorded the traditions and tales of Mabon, and there are indeed some parallels between Mabon's story, as summarized in the tale of *Culhwch and Olwen*, and the story of the birth and adventures of Pryderi, who appears in the First, Third, and Fourth Branches and whose name appears in the Second, though he is not in any simple sense the 'hero' of any of the four. It may be, of course, that both of the above theories contain some truth, for words shift their meanings, carry multiple meanings, and frequently outgrow their etymologies.

The use of *mabinogi* in the colophon to the Third Branch is anomalous and thus difficult to interpret: 'And because of that imprisonment, that tale is called *Mabinogi of Collar and Yoke*' (p. 76). Any precise meaning for *mabinogi* in this context is elusive; it may be a generic term for a tale, or for a particular type of tale, or for one of the specific tales or episodes embedded in this collection. The colophon then concludes with the statement familiar from the other three branches: 'And thus ends this branch of *The Mabinogi*,' once again in a clear reference to the Four Branches as a whole.

The titles at the head of each branch are translated from the rubrics in the *Red Book of Hergest*. For the first one, I have added the definite article 'the' where the Red Book reads *Llyma dechreu Mabinogi* 'Here begins (a) *Mabinogi*.' There is some debate whether this refers to the entire *Mabinogi* or just the First Branch, but the rubrics of the remaining three branches all include the definite article. Thus the preponderance of the manuscript evidence points to *The Mabinogi* as the collective title of the four branches. This is also the title understood by Dr John Davies in his table of contents of the *White Book*, written c.1634: '*Y mabinogi. Mewn 28 o ddalenau*' ('The mabinogi. On 28 leaves'). Many scholars and translators use the title *The Four Branches of the Mabinogi*. While this is perfectly descriptive of the existing texts, it is a modern convention, and I have chosen to use the shorter alternative on the weight of the manuscript evidence. It has also become standard modern practice to refer to each of the branches by the name of one of its main characters – Pwyll, Branwen, Manawydan, and Math. However, in the absence of any early evidence of this practice, and unwilling to imply that any one character is the main figure in each branch, I have chosen not to use these names as titles, but to refer to each branch by number, as does Hywel Fychan, the scribe of the *Red Book of Hergest*.

Further Reading

This short bibliography is not complete; it is meant simply to direct the interested reader to some of the most important studies in English of *The Mabinogi* and related topics.

Editions:

The following editions of the Welsh texts of the Four Branches have proved indispensable in preparing this translation:

Williams, Ifor. *Pedeir Keinc y Mabinogi.* Caerdydd, 1961. The standard edition of the Welsh text. [In Welsh]

Thompson, R. L. *Pwyll Pendeuic Dyuet.* Dublin, 1957.

Thomson, Derick S. *Branwen Uerch Lyr.* Dublin, 1961.

Ford, Patrick K. *Manawydan uab Llyr.* Belmont, Massachusetts, 2000.

Ford, Patrick K. *Math uab Mathonwy.* Belmont, Massachusetts, 1999.

Hughes, Ian. *Math Uab Mathonwy.* Aberystwyth, 2000. [In Welsh]

Studies and Surveys:

Sullivan, C. W., III. *The Mabinogi: A Book of Essays.* New York, 1996. A collection of sixteen major scholarly articles on *The Mabinogi* that were published between 1970 and 1990.

Davies, Sioned. *The Four Branches of the Mabinogi.* Llandysul, 1993. A brief but important introduction, with particular attention to the oral tradition that underlies the tales.

Mac Cana, Proinsias. *The Mabinogi.* Cardiff, 1977. A perceptive and influential discussion of the Four Branches and other tales in the 'Mabinogion.'

Jackson, Kenneth. *The International Popular Tale and Early Welsh Tradition.* Cardiff, 1961.

Mac Cana, Proinsias. *Branwen Daughter of Llŷr: A Study of the Irish Affinities and of the Composition of the Second Branch of the Mabinogi.* Cardiff, 1958.

Gruffydd, W. J. *Rhiannon: An Inquiry into the First and Third Branches of the Mabinogi.* Cardiff, 1953.

Related Reading:

Bromwich, Rachel. *Trioedd Ynys Prydein: The Welsh Triads.* Cardiff, 1961, 1978.

Green, Miranda Jane. *Celtic Myths.* London, 1993.

Green, Miranda J. *Dictionary of Celtic Myth and Legend.* London, 1992.

Mac Cana, Proinsias. *Celtic Mythology.* London, 1970.

Rees, Alwyn, and Brinley Rees. *Celtic Heritage.* London 1961.

INDEX

of Proper Names in *The Mabinogi*

A Note on Welsh Pronunciation

This index includes pronunciation respellings for all the Welsh names in *The Mabinogi*. Following these guidelines should allow you to produce a pronunciation acceptable to Welsh speakers.

The names and Welsh words appearing in this translation are given in modern Welsh spelling. Though it may look strange to English readers, Welsh spelling is quite regular, with far fewer rules and exceptions than in English. Most Welsh vowels and diphthongs are pronounced much as they are in continental European languages. The consonants are generally pronounced as in English, with a few notable exceptions.

The stressed or emphatic syllable in Welsh words of more than one syllable is almost always the next-to-last syllable. Stress is indicated in the respellings by **boldface** type.

The most famous – or most notorious – Welsh sound is represented by *ll*. Pronounce *ll* with the tongue in the same position as for the *l* in *lady* by blowing air past the side of the tongue, without voice (as if whispering). It will sound like a hiss. Don't be hesitant; give a good, forceful, blow. The *l* in English *clean* is very similar.

In Welsh the letter *w* can represent both a consonant sound, as in English *win* and *twice*, or the vowel sounds of *pool* and *pull*. (Note that *w* also serves a vowel function in English, as in *law* and *crowd*.)

Key to Pronunciation Symbols

Vowel and Diphthong Symbols

$\|\breve{a}\|$ = *a* in *father, starry*	$\|\hat{o}\|$ = *o* in *cross*
$\|au\|$ = *ou* in *now*	$\|\bar{o}\|$ = *o* in *go*
$\|e\|$ = *e* in *bed, berry*	$\|oi\|$ = *oi* in *coin*
$\|\bar{e}\|$ = *ee* in *seed*	$\|oo\|$ = *oo* in *soon, good*
$\|i\|$ = *i* in *sit*	$\|u\|$ = *u* in *put, good, poor*
$\|\bar{i}\|$ = *i* in *ride, aisle*	$\|u\bar{e}\|$ = *ooey* in *pho**oey***
	$\|ui\|$ = *o i* in "*You can do it*"
	$\|uh\|$ = *a, o* in *above*

Consonant Symbols

$\|g\|$ = *g* in *go*	$\|r\|$: *r* is generally trilled
$\|hr\|$: Pronounce both $\|h\|$ and $\|r\|$	$\|th\|$ = *th* in *thin, bath*
$\|kh\|$ = *ch* in Scottish *loch*	$\|\underline{th}\|$ = *th* in *this, bathe*
$\|ll\|$: as explained above	$\|w\|$ = *w* in *with, twice*

The 12th-century Cistercian
abbey at Strata Florida (Ystrad
Fflur), where the *White Book of
Rhydderch* was probably written,
became the most important
abbey in Wales. The foundations
of its walls and the Norman arch
of the great west doorway
testify to its former glory.